Memoirs

OF A

First Lady

(Through the Journals of Her Life)

C.D. COVINGTON

ISBN 978-1-0980-2536-6 (paperback)
ISBN 978-1-0980-2537-3 (digital)

Christian Faith Publishing, Inc.
832 Park Avenue
Meadville, PA 16335
www.christianfaithpublishing.com

Printed in the United States of America

Those who let themselves be controlled by their lower natures live only to please themselves, but those who follow after the Holy Spirit finds themselves doing those things that pleases God.

—Romans 8:5, TLB

PREFACE

Often, I remember the smell of great grandmother's house back in the '60s when breakfast was the biggest meal of the day. If I close my eyes and reflect, I can smell fresh brewed coffee cooking in one of those stove-top percolator with the cute little glass handle on top. Sniff closer, and I might smell bacon cooking, with rice and home-made biscuits.

Great grandmother's motto was "Eat breakfast like a king, lunch like a queen, and dinner like a peasant." These are Southern qualities most cherished and remembered, just like the pages in this memoir you are about to read.

These are lovely cherished stories about loving and looking for love. In that search, there is a mixture of adultery, hurt, and betrayal. There is also beauty and growth. What is this memoir about, you ask? An insider's perspective about cheating, hurt, and disappointment within the church. It's also about finding and loving your soul mate. There is no male bashing or intended demeaning of women. This is just a nonfictional collection of events portrayed by fictional characters.

This is a fictional story with just a hint of truth that it might remind you of someone you know. Any resemblance to real life is purely coincidental. Whatever the case may be, human attraction is a very real emotion, and human flaws can cause some to do things they never thought possible. Travel with us on this journey with this small-town country girl raised in South Georgia on good old-fashion southern values, who got caught in the middle of lust, love, and deception within the church.

JOURNAL 1

The Introduction

No temptation has overtaken you except what is common to mankind. And God is faithful; He will not let you be tempted beyond what you can bear.

—1 Corinthians 10:13 (NLV)

Da'nessa Baker is a lovely Christian girl. There is something alluring about her physically and spiritually. She is African American with smooth mocha coffee-skin tone. She stands about five feet two inches tall and is always wearing high-heel shoes. Da'nessa has beautiful bone structure and lovely thick hair, like her great grandmother, Ma Bessie.

Da'nessa believes that her hometown is just too small to contain her sense of adventure. It's 1980; she has just finished high school, and she is ready to see the world. She searches for an escape route to travel and explore the world. She knows there is more to see than farmland, dirt roads, and small-town groceries stores.

The military is her ticket to see the world according to all those great commercials they show on television. She imagines herself onboard one of those big naval ships in the middle of the ocean, watching the waves bouncing off the water. What a beautiful picture she has painted in her mind. Da'nessa loves the water. As a child, she cherished those summer trips to the Florida beaches with her family in that old blue Ford station wagon.

As it turns out, her cousin is dating a local navy recruiter who has been bugging her to join the Navy and see the world. After much consideration, she decided she would enlist in the United States Navy.

Da'nessa grew up in the church. Therefore, when she entered the navy, she continued to go to church faithfully. Her first duty station was on the island of Guam. How blessed to have an exotic island as your first job assignment. She just considered herself lucky to be surrounded by all of that beautiful water. Da'nessa had been stationed on Guam six months when her life changed forever.

Rupert Latimore is an officer in the United States Air Force. He serves as a chaplain on Anderson Air Force Base. He is the only African American chaplain on the island. Rupert is an attractive man and a very kind person. People seem to naturally like him. By all accounts, Rupert is a happily married man. He and his wife Cynthia Latimore have been married for eight years. They have no children because both seem so focused on their careers. She is a nurse and works long hours. They have discussed having kids, but Cynthia is not keen on the idea. Cynthia comes from a large family where she always had to share. She despised having to share anything now that she is grown. Growing up, Cynthia's family was poor. Her parents would always seek donations from local churches and other charitable organizations. She and her siblings were often teased because they wore used clothing. This created such a sore spot in her heart. Cynthia became materialist and only wanted the newest and best items. You would never catch her in a thrift store or a consignment shop.

Rupert, on the other hand, was born with a sliver spoon in his mouth. He is one of two boys. Rupert is a mommy's boy. He was named after his grandfather who died on the morning of his birth. Some said his grandfather gave up his spirit so that Rupert could enter the world and continue the great work that his grandfather so loved. Rupert's grandfather was a minister. Grandfather Latimore is a well-loved and highly respected person. He set the standard for the men in his family. It was no surprise that Rupert was expected to follow the career path of the "Cloth." In other words, he became a minister. He always seemed to do the right thing. The expectations were high, and Rupert lived up to them.

Rupert is a tall man standing about six feet three inches and weighing about 230 pounds. Rupert works out at the gym almost daily. He is handsome with a light-skinned complexion and a toned beautiful body. At first glance, one would think he is Hispanic, but he is quick to correct anyone that he is 100 percent African American/ Black.

This good-looking man meets beautiful women all the time but never once allowed them beyond the point of his profession. Women of all nationalities find him attractive. There are some that openly flirts with him and are not afraid to make their intentions known. He politely rejects them.

He has a strong sense of awareness to his commitment to God. Rupert has the highest regards for his wife's feelings and his grandfather's standards when faced with temptation. He had a big reputation to live up to emulating his grandfather, and he has been determined to do so from an early age. Rupert strives daily to be a faithful husband and a good Christian. By all accounts, he has been considered such a person until one day, by chance on a beach, on the island of Guam, his entire life changed.

JOURNAL 2

First Encounter

*For Those who live according to the flesh set their
minds on the things of the flesh, but those who live
according to the Spirit, the things of the Spirit.*

—Romans 8:5 (NKJV)

It was a warm sunny day and everyone was hanging out at Tarague Beach on Anderson Air Force Base, Guam, located on the north end of the island. The smell of char-grilled burgers and hotdogs filled the air. There's loud music playing from various sound systems. The sound of "Upside Down" by singer Diana Ross blasted from the speaker systems. Apparently, the radio station loved this song as much as the beachgoers because they played it about every other hour.

Volleyball was the primary sports game at the beach. Today was no exception; there were games throughout the landscape. Those not playing were lying around on beach towels watching or just enjoying the sun. Rupert was highly competitive when it came to sports, and to him, the only option was to win. He won often, and if by chance he lost, he showed great sportsmanship and congratulated the winners. He was not a poor sport; he just liked winning.

Today Rupert had been engrossed in a serious game of volleyball. It was sudden death, and both teams had fourteen points each, and his team had the advantage of the serve. The final serve of the game was tossed, and luckily it was Rupert doing the serving. He was the best server on the team. The other team returned the serve, and the volley of the ball went back and forth. This was not unusual. As a matter of fact, it was expected because Rupert's friends and coworkers were just as competitive.

Finally, the smash hit that sealed the win happened. When Rupert came down on the volleyball with his fist, he was careful not to hit the net. The game was over, and his team won. There was cheering and shouts of joy. Team members were very busy high-fiving one another for the victory. In the midst of celebrating, no one realized that the small white volleyball had left the court and wondered over near a small group of secluded rocks.

Da'nessa lay quietly on her towel in her favorite spot on the beach amongst the secluded rocks. It was a location somewhat away from the main activities on the beach but close enough to feel and hear the sounds of the ocean. She loved this location. It offered what she needed most: seclusion and a good place to lie and read one of her favorite books. She loved to read, and on this warm day, she was reading a romance novel.

Da'nessa was so into her characters that she didn't seem to notice the volleyball that had gently rolled into her space. It seems to just lie there and observe her reading. No one came to claim it, and she seemed to ignore it. There they were both in the same space and time, yet unaware that either existed. Hours seem to pass by when, finally, Da'nessa emerged from her romance novel. The beach seemed to have quieted, and some of its occupants had abandoned it. Then she saw it, the smooth white ball that seemed to have appeared out of nowhere.

Rupert had forgotten the volleyball and returned to the beach to retrieve it. It was his responsibility because, after all, he was the one who had borrowed it from the youth department at the Air Force Base chapel. He had searched for at least ten minutes. Trying to recall where he had last seen the small white ball. Maybe a kid found it and took it home, he thought. If he didn't locate it soon, he would have to go to the local sports store and just replace the ball.

He was normally more responsible. This was so out of character for him. He would have surely stored the ball safely in his truck after the game. Then returned it back to the youth department. This was not the first time he had borrowed a volleyball. This was the first time he had failed to put it away in his truck after the game.

Da'nessa picked up the ball and felt a slight connection. There was something very spiritual about her. Da'nessa had known this since childhood. There was a realm that she operated in that most people were unaware. She was once told by her great grandmother that she was born with a veil. Which is a caul, a piece of the sac that breaks away during the birth process and attaches itself to the baby's face. Many cultures consider this a sign of good luck. Some call it a sort of sixth sense.

When she picked up the ball, she thought that some sad little kid had lost it and was probably home upset over it. She purposed in her mind to take it to the lifeguard station, just in case the child returned to look for it. As she emerged from her secluded location with her new friend, the volleyball, Rupert saw her, and something inside his heart skipped a beat. Strangely, he felt a soul connection to her instantly. Rupert felt a deja' vu connection to her, as if he knew her from another place and time.

She hadn't noticed him yet, but he had surely seen her. Something about her seems so familiar. *That's impossible*, he thought, because he had never seen her in his life. Had it been so, he would have remembered! What is it about her that caused his mind to admire and analyze her? He didn't feel any type of lust; just an odd sort of attraction.

She was dressed modestly. He knew she had on a bathing suit, but she had it covered with a yellow sundress-type garment. She had her hair swept up in a loose bun and didn't appear to have on any makeup. Cynthia would never go without makeup in public, he thought.

The young lady was carrying a volleyball that appeared to be like the one he was looking for, but he didn't want to assume it was his. Volleyballs are such a common thing. Maybe this ball belonged to her child. Was she old enough to have a child? he thought. She appeared to be in her early twenties, maybe twenty-one or twenty-two but not older than that. Here he was on the beach thinking about another woman. Why had she taken up this much of his thoughts?

As Da'nessa walked down the beach headed toward the lifeguard tower, she noticed Rupert. He appeared to be walking toward her with a bewildered look on his face. He had not known that she could read his facial expressions. Their eyes met, and she looked deep and hard into them. The look made him feel as if she had just peeped into his very soul. He had no idea how correct his thoughts were. She had indeed looked into his very soul, and what she saw was sadness. She also noticed the wedding ring he was wearing. She smiled at him, as she always did when approaching someone. She was a Southern girl from South Georgia and was taught to always be polite.

"Excuse me," said Rupert, "but is that your volleyball? I seem to have misplaced mine."

Da'nessa smiled and simply replied, "I seem to have found one that was misplaced."

She playfully asked him to describe his lost volleyball because she wanted to make sure he was the rightful owner. Rupert smiled. She has a sense of humor, he thought to himself. He liked that in a person. He decided to play along and described his volleyball as being round, white, and firm to the touch. "Correct description," said Da'nessa, then she handed the ball over to him.

Rupert then introduced himself by first name only to her. She in return told him her first name. He thanked her for returning the ball, and they both walked toward the parking area making small talk as they went along. Both commented on how beautiful the beach was late in the day. She told him that she liked that it was quite, with very few people as the sun was beginning to set. It was nearing sundown. Da'nessa got into her small blue Toyota Corolla, waved goodbye, and drove away. She thought to herself, *Too bad, he is married.*

Rupert sat in his truck at the beach for a long time just thinking about life. Then he decided to get out and return to the beach for a walk. He could not get the thought of Da'nessa out of his mind. Why had such a nice person lingered in his thoughts? Why was he thinking about another woman? This was so unlike him. He is a married man with a wife at home. Rupert decided to have a conversation with God. "Father God," he started off his prayer, "please cleanse me of my thoughts about Da'nessa. Help me to focus on my responsibilities as a minister and as a husband to my wife." The prayer continues, "Father, I met Da'nessa on this beach, help me to leave the thoughts of her here on this beach. I need your strength to do this." He had hoped his prayer would help, but his flesh appeared to be stronger for the moment, and he continued to think about the way she looked into his very soul.

As Da'nessa drove toward the naval facility where she resided, she tried to remain focus on other things, but Rupert kept popping up in her mind. She told herself that he is a married man, and it is forbidden to think about him. She is a Christian, and she recognized sinful thoughts. Thoughts such as desiring a married man is adultery, even if you have not slept together. The mere thought is wrong. Da'nessa has been in church long enough to know this. She wanted no part of adultery.

Da'nessa knew a few things about strong mind control. She was keenly aware that thoughts can produce actions, even unwanted and ungodly actions. She decided to play praise-and-worship music on her radio as she continued her drive home. Life proceeded on as normal for the both of them.

JOURNAL 3

We Meet Again

A friend loves at all times.

—Proverbs 17:7 (NKJV)

Rosemary Thomas is Da'nessa's best friend on the island of Guam. They met in basic military training school and instantly became friends. Rosemary had recently divorced her husband of three years and was doing some serious soul-searching. The divorce had been bitter. She often relied on Da'nessa to vent and offer words of comfort. They had often attended church together on the naval base.

One Saturday, out of the blue, Rosemary asked Da'nessa to go with her to check out the church service on the Air Force base. She had heard wonderful things about the service there on fourth Sunday. She was told that the service was like that of the Baptist churches back home. Rosemary loved a good Baptist service. Da'nessa had grown up Methodist and was used to the traditional ways of doing things. She was okay with the Catholic service on the naval base, but Rosemary had always complained. Da'nessa wanted to be supportive of her friend, so she agreed to go to the Air Force base church with her on Sunday.

The parking area was full, which surprised both of them. They were not aware that such a large number of people attended church

15

service like this. Rosemary commented to Da'nessa that it must be a good service. They finally found a parking spot in the overflow parking area. It was a good walk to the church door, but they were young and in good shape.

Rupert was having an emotional morning. He and Cynthia, his wife, had an argument that morning. She had volunteered to work a shift at the naval hospital for a coworker. Normally, Rupert didn't mind, but today was different. She knew that it was his Sunday to speak in church. Cynthia had started to slack off from church attendance. She had clearly replaced God with a monetary one. She loved her salary and all the attention it awarded her. She drove a beautiful Mercedes Benz special ordered from the United States.

Their home was a showpiece. Although they lived in military housing, it was the officers' military housing. The Air Force spared no expense when it came to their facilities, and housing was no exception. Cynthia loved to show off. It made her feel important for once in her life. Having grown up in a large family, she was never the center of attention. No one was the center of attention in her family. She often thought that the only reason her father had kids was to assist with the financial responsibilities of a large family.

Everyone in her family had to work part-time jobs and share the family's expenses. Now that she had the opportunity to be somebody, there was no way she was going to share the spotlight, especially not tied down to raising children. Rupert would have to understand for now. In her mind, he had always had more than his fair share of attention. He should be more understanding of her needs, she thought.

Rupert decided to shift his thinking off of Cynthia and focus more on his pending sermon. God had given him a great topic to share. One he felt his wife needed to hear. He knew he had to record the sermon on his tape recorder and play it later so that maybe she will hear it and change her ways. His sermon topic for today is taken from the book of Exodus in the Bible located in chapter 20, verse 3, that states, "Thy shall have no other gods before Me." God First.

From the pastor's office intercom, Rupert could hear the praise and worship team singing. He loves to hear them sing, but following protocol, he remained in his study until the deacons (church volunteer staff) complete opening prayer. He glanced out the window and noticed that it appeared to be a large crowd this morning. He was mainly looking to see if Cynthia's car was in her reserved parking spot. Maybe she will surprise him, but it was after 10:00 a.m., and her spot remained empty. Things in the chapel got quiet. Prayer time. He knew that was his clue to proceed to the church sanctuary. When the opening prayer was over, the church secretary got up and asked all visitors to please stand.

Rosemary and Da'nessa stood along with about twenty other guests. Then the secretary introduced Pastor Rupert Latimore. "He will be saying a few words of welcome," she stated. They asked the guests to remain standing. As he had done so many times before, Pastor Rupert walked up to the podium to welcome the guest. He scanned the crowd as usual.

Then he stopped to his left toward this one section of the church. His heart skipped a beat. He thought to himself, *Is it really her?* For a long moment, he paused as if he had forgotten what to say next. He looked again, and this time her eyes caught his. They both smiled, and he was then able to move on with the welcome.

Pastor Rupert's sermon went very well on the surface, but inside he struggled. How can he think about this other woman in the middle of a sermon? A sermon especially designed by God for his wife to hear. His wife Cynthia who was not even in attendance! The church was filled to the overflow room. Da'nessa looked around trying to decipher which female was his wife. For some strange reason, she had hoped he would introduce his wife or at least acknowledge her presence during the service. There was no real reason for him to do so. She just wanted him to for her sake. She wanted to know who the lucky woman is to win such a handsome and accomplished man.

When they had met on the beach, she would never have known he was a pastor. Her mind was wondering back to that day they met. She heard her inside voice speaking to her: *Focus on his sermon and stop daydreaming about this married pastor. Besides, he may not remember you, so why waste time thinking about him?* That's what she told herself as she sat in the service. If the truth be told, they were both thinking about one another.

After service, it was customary that the pastor greets the visitors as they exit the church. He would thank them for attending and invite them to come back again. As the visitors stood in line to exit the church and greet the pastor, Rosemary whispered to Da'nessa how handsome she thought the pastor was. "Too bad, he is married," she commented.

Da'nessa didn't say a word and hoped that her nervousness didn't show. *He would never remember me,* she said to herself again. Rosemary extended her hand to shake the pastor's hand. He welcomed her and asked if she enjoyed the service. He could tell they were together and was unsure if Da'nessa remembered him. He decided to be open and up-front. He reached for Da'nessa's hand and said, "Hello, Da'nessa, it's nice to see you again." She in return said, "Hello, Pastor Rupert. It's nice to see you also." Rosemary was shocked, to say the least. The two of them continued in light conversation. He thanked them for attending.

She and Rosemary departed the church toward the parking lot. Out of hearing range of the church, Rosemary turned to Da'nessa and asked, "Why didn't you tell me, your best friend, that you knew the pastor?" Da'nessa laughed. "I didn't know that I knew the pastor."

"Well, he seems to know your name," said Rosemary.

"We met about three weeks ago at the beach," Da'nessa explained. "I found a volleyball and was about to turn it into the lifeguard when he approached me about it. It was his volleyball, and he had been searching for it. I didn't know he was a pastor. Let alone the pastor here at the Air Force base. We briefly introduced ourselves, and I gave him the volleyball, and we parted ways. I had not seen him again until today. I was shocked, plus I didn't think he would even remember me."

"Well, he did remember you," exclaimed Rosemary with a hint of jealousy in her voice.

"Anyway, the man is married," said Da'nessa.

"Married or not, he remembered your name," snorted Rosemary.

"Let's forget about it and go home," stated Da'nessa, who was trying to appear cool, calm, and collected to her friend. Inside, Da'nessa was extremely flattered.

It had been at least two months since Da'nessa attended church service at Anderson AFB with Rosemary. Rosemary had returned the next fourth Sunday, but Da'nessa chose not to. She didn't want to see Pastor Rupert because he always gave her the feeling of butterflies in her stomach. She didn't want to feed in to her desires for this married man.

It was late Sunday evening a few hours before sunset. It was midsummer by now, and the days were long. Da'nessa decided to go spend some time at the beach. Because it was late in the day, only a few people were at the beach. Da'nessa had a new romance novel she wanted to read. She loved reading at the beach and listening to the sound of the ocean in the background. She had even purchased one of those sound machines that mimic the sound of the oceans, birds, and the forest, but it wasn't the same as experiencing it in person. She figured this time of day, most families with kids will be leaving, and only the true adult beach lovers will be there. Da'nessa was correct. There were a few scattered lovers lying around soaking up the last few rays of sun. She wasn't there for the sun. Her coffee-mocha skin didn't need any more sun. She always found herself in the small outcrop of rocks shaded from the sun but in full range of the sound of the oceans.

It was a sweet sound hearing the waters racing back and forth over the sand. Intermingling as it crashed and bounced off the rocks. She often pictured it as various spirits dancing and intertwining in a passionate embrace. Da'nessa knew that she was hopelessly romantic. It's a strange way to think of the ocean, but it's the image that she had created in her mind, and she loved it. The thought was pure and sensual. Da'nessa was so deep in thought that she had not noticed his approach. He cleared his throat to get her attention. "Hello, may I interrupt you for a moment," said a strong familiar male voice. She looked up and saw Pastor Rupert standing over her in an almost regal manner.

"Hello," she replied, "please take a seat" was all she could manage to get out. He seemed happy and eager to take her up on the offer. Da'nessa blushed as he sat down to join her. He noticed her shyness and was all the more impressed by this lovely person.

"Where is your hometown, Da'nessa?" he asked, trying to make small talk.

"I'm from a small town in South Georgia called Adel. Where are you from?" she asked in return.

"I'm from Kansas City, Missouri," was his reply. She had heard of Kansas City but never met anyone from there. Let alone anyone black. "Why are you alone on the beach yet again?" he asked. He was really fishing to see if she was married or in a committed relationship.

Da'nessa is very wise and knew how to play this game of secret inquiry. She decided to be straightforward with him. "I'm single, not married, and currently not in a relationship. I love spending time alone reading and relaxing when I'm not on duty with the United States Navy." In a nutshell, she just admitted to being a reclusive military geek. "What about you, Pastor Rupert?" she said.

He chuckled. "A straight shooter, huh! First of all, please just call me Rupert," he said. "Yes, I'm married. I married my high school sweetheart. Her name is Cynthia, and she is a nurse at naval hospital." He wasn't sure why he shared so much information with her. Yet, he felt as if he could trust her, tell her everything, and she would listen with her full attention focused on him.

Da'nessa smiled and looked deep into his eyes. "Why are you so sad?" she asked. She didn't know why she felt the need to ask him that. Maybe she wanted to impress him with her insight, but then again, something inside her cared and was concerned for his sadness.

Rupert looked at Da'nessa with amazement. He decided he could totally trust her enough to open up some of his pain to her. "Things are not so great at home. I want my wife to have a child, hopefully a baby boy. My wife doesn't want kids. She will not openly admit it, but I can read between the lines." He rambled on, "My wife comes from a large family. Her career is her life and substitute baby, which I can't nurture or take a part in its development. I have been praying and asking God how to handle this ache in my soul." *Wow, why am I babbling on?* he thought.

Da'nessa was sorry she had asked. Now she really connected to him in such an affectionate manner. She wishes she could take him in her arms and hold him until everything was all right. How do you alleviate emotional pain for a married man, let alone a married pastor, a man of God? Da'nessa offered the only thing she knew how to offer, a prayer, "Let's touch and agree in prayer that God will soon work this out for you and your wife." Rupert was impressed: a young woman who believed in the power of prayer.

Da'nessa enjoyed his company for that next few hours, but as the sun went down, she knew it was time to say goodbye. Rupert walked her to her car. He wanted very much to ask for her phone number, but he knew best in his heart not to. He is a married man, and she is a single woman. They said their goodbye and parted ways.

Pastor Rupert came to the beach several times over the next couple of Sundays. He would always come late in the day hoping to run into Da'nessa. She, on the other hand, stayed away from the beach because she knew in her heart she longed to see him and spend time in his company. Her upbringing had taught her that this type of relationship was forbidden. She would often remind herself that it was a sin to think upon a married man, especially a man serving God in the pulpit. She often thought of the scripture, Psalm 105:15: "Touch not my anointed one" (paraphrased). She aimed to get this scripture right among others. So she did all within her power to avoid him.

JOURNAL 4

Dealing with Disappointment

*Man who is born of woman is of few days
and full of trouble.*

—Job 14:1 (NKJV)

Cynthia was not looking forward to flying home for the funeral. She knew very well that as a daughter-in-law, she would be expected. It was her wifely duty. Rupert was in deep grief and pain. He had just lost his beloved mother. No pain in the entire world could have prepared him for this loss. She was his best friend and confidant. He loved and respected his mother, but he also shared a counseling bond with her. She would keep his deepest fears and concerns to herself. He shared things with his mother that he never shared with another soul, not even his father whom he is very close to.

He knew Cynthia was not there for him emotionally. She was disconnected from anything outside of herself. He was carrying too much pain to be concerned with her selfishness at this time. He made all the arrangements and booked their flight back to the United States. It was late Monday, and their flight would not depart until Wednesday. Flights to the United States only departed the island on Monday, Wednesday, and Friday. It's a small island, and there was no need for daily flights, plus the local officials were very conscious of the environment and insisted upon an eco-friendly existence.

Cynthia, on the other hand, had accepted work on a midnight shift for Tuesday night. She waited until the last minute on Tuesday to tell Rupert. She swore that there was no one to call to replace her. She apologized and tried to fake her concerns. She promised to meet Rupert at the airport that Wednesday morning. Rupert was disappointed that she would work at all, considering his beloved mother had passed away. He knew that Cynthia and his mother didn't care much for one another. His mother was against the marriage, and Cynthia knew it. She said that Cynthia's spirit was not right. She knew Cynthia had a strong love for material things, and she sensed her selfishness. He married her anyway, hoping that his mom would understand just how much he loved Cynthia's faults and all. Rupert gave Cynthia her plane ticket information and went to bed. He mourned deeply. He mourned for the loss of his mother, and he mourned for the comfort of his wife. Both were now missing in his life.

The airport smelled of cinnamon buns and coffee. It wasn't a very busy airport, but on flight days, people were coming and going, giving the appearance of a busy airport. On certain days, the Air Force would land one of their military hops, a plan flight that included military families seeking a vacation in the flight's destination. This activity would really give the impression that it was a busy airport.

It was two hours before boarding time, and Cynthia had not arrived at the airport. Rupert kept a watchful eye out for her, but she still had not arrived. Forty-five minutes before the flight boarding was to begin, Rupert was paged over the intercom to the check-in desk. The airport staff said he had an emergency phone call. Knowing it was most likely Cynthia, he answered the phone with an attitude. Hearing a strange voice on the other end, he released his anger toward Cynthia and replaced it with concern. "Pastor Latimore, this is Nurse McCartney calling from Naval Facility Hospital," said the voice on the other end of the phone. Rupert's heart dropped; he was sure something had happened to Cynthia. It was a staff member from the hospital where she worked. He could not take any additional sad news. It took all he had to remain composed.

He asked the nurse if this is concerning his wife Cynthia. "Is everything okay?"

The voice on the other end replied, "Everything is fine. I don't mean to alarm you. Your wife asked me to relay a message. She is still in the operating room and will miss the flight. She promises to be on the evening flight, and she had me to change her reservations. She said she will see you in Kansas City and will phone you later." Then the nurse said have a safe flight and goodbye.

Rupert was livid, to say the least. This was the final straw in her hat of selfishness. How can she be so insensitive to his needs? In his mind, she could stoop no lower. He needed her most, and she let him down. He thought, *Dear God, what kind of woman did I marry? My mother was right.* Then he spoke a soft message toward heaven to his mother, "Mom, if you can hear me from heaven, you were right about Cynthia. I never should have married her."

Another announcement came over the intercom. "We are now boarding Flight 1326 to San Francisco, CA. Passengers with seats on row P through Z may board at this time, and first-class passengers may board at your convenience." Rupert was so upset with Cynthia that he had not noticed one person boarding the plane. With his head down trying not to cry over the insensitive behavior of his wife, he didn't hear the boarding staff call him softly. "Pastor Rupert, we are making the final boarding call." He picked up his things and headed for his seat in first-class. Rupert had decided he was going to sleep the entire flight back to the United States. Which was a twelve-hour flight. Rupert's mind was racing with all kinds of thoughts. Now he ran the risk of some stranger sitting next to him because his wife had conveniently changed her ticket. If there was such a thing as a pastor hating his wife, well he currently hated Cynthia.

Rupert prayed silently, "Lord, give me a better spirit and remove this anger. Don't let me be bitter all the way home on this flight." He then closed his eyes and fell asleep. About an hour into his flight, Rupert awoke to the smell of coffee, toast, and bacon.

The first-class flight attendant noticed he was awake and asked if he wanted breakfast or something to drink, such as coffee, tea, or juice. Rupert asked for coffee and a breakfast tray with toast, bacon, and egg. He noticed that no one was sitting next to him. The flight was not a full one, and there were other empty seats in first-class. Meanwhile, in the coach section of the plane, there was a problem with one of the restrooms, so the line was starting to back up. The head flight attendant made a decision to open up one of the first-class restrooms to everyone. Rupert had gotten up to use the restroom. He was still somewhat groggy from the events of the morning and had planned to wash his face and freshen up.

He stood for a few seconds waiting for the last person to exit the restroom. Da'nessa walked out. Shocked and somewhat surprised he was glad to see her. It had been at least two months since they had seen one another. Da'nessa was equally as shocked to see him. They said good morning to one another. Da'nessa returned to her seat amazed that they were on the same flight. She thought to herself, *Maybe I can finally see what his wife looks like.*

Rupert freshened up in the restroom and wondered if Da'nessa was on the flight alone. When he exited the restroom, he searched all over first-class but did not see her sitting anywhere. Then he thought maybe he had imagined her there. He knew that grief can do strange things to a person. Maybe in his grief, he wanted to see a comforting soul such as Da'nessa. He returned to his seat and ate his breakfast. Rupert was unaware that people from the coach section of the plane were using the first-class restroom. He thought about asking the flight attendant if she was on board, but he remembered he had never asked her for her last name.

Rupert finish his breakfast and thought about Da'nessa for a long time before finally dosing off to sleep again. Da'nessa sat in coach wondering what Pastor Rupert's wife looked like. Was she tall and beautiful like a model? Maybe she's short with a beautiful shape. She pictured her as elegant. The model type with a beautiful short haircut and manicured nails. Cynthia is the perfect model type in Da'nessa's mind. Ministers and pastors seem to always marry beautiful women. They need showpieces by their side to prove that God blesses them for their service—the trophy wife or so that is the gossip among church folk. After all, the wives do become "first ladies"; they are like royalty in church circles.

Rupert got up to asked for a warm moist towel from the flight staff. That's when he saw her again. She was sitting in coach. He also noticed that people from coach were using the restroom in first-class. Why had he not noticed that before and put two and two together? Anyway, wanting to talk to her, he approached her seat. She was sitting next to another lady, and it was clear to him that she was on this flight alone. "Hello, Da'nessa, how is your flight so far?" he asked. She was surprised that he had approached her seat, especially with his wife somewhere on board. She assumed he just wanted to make a little small talk. She responded by calling him Pastor Rupert. He managed a smile and said, "I thought we had agreed that you would just call me Rupert."

There were some small turbulences on the plane and the captain lit the fasten seat belt sign. Everyone was asked to return to their seat; Rupert said goodbye and returned to first-class. He sat in his seat for about ten minutes; he pushed the button for the flight attendant. Rupert explained to her that a friend of his was in coach, and they haven't seen one another in a while. Since someone was sitting next to her, he asked if it was okay if she joins him in first-class. He knew the plane was not full. He even offered to pay for a ticket upgrade. The flight attendant said it was okay if both parties agreed.

Rupert returned to the coach section. Da'nessa had dozed off to sleep. He tapped her on the shoulders. When she opened her eyes, they seemed to light up when she noticed it was him. He asked her softly if she would like to join him in first-class. He said he had cleared it with the flight staff. "What about your wife?" she asked. "I'm on this flight alone. Please join me," he pleaded. She agreed and reached in the overhead to get her carry-on case. Rupert assisted her with the case, and they returned to his seat. He offered her the window seat. The seats in first-class were big and comfortable. The flight staff came and asked if either of them wanted something to eat or drink. Da'nessa asked for a cup of hot tea, and Rupert asked for water.

Rupert asked Da'nessa was she traveling on official military business. She answered no. Then she told him of her plans to attend her great grandmother's eighty-fifth birthday celebration. Da'nessa then turned to him and asked the same question. Why was he flying back to the States? He said with sadness in his eyes, "I'm going home to bury my mother. She died this past Sunday."

Da'nessa was sorry she asked. She expressed her condolences. Then she did something totally unexpected. She lifted the armrest between them and reached out and embraced him in her arms. She held him next to her soft bosom. She felt his tears flow as she wrapped him in her arms. Rupert needed so much to be held, and Da'nessa was there in that moment holding him.

When the flight attendant returned, she asked if everything was okay. They assured her it was okay. Then she brought them over a package of tissue to wipe their eyes. After about fifteen minutes, Rupert pulled himself together and drank some of his water. Da'nessa looked intently in his eyes searching for the right moment and words for such a time as this. Then she decided to just keep silent. She learned a long time ago that sometimes it best to just keep silent. Rupert knew at that moment he needed and wanted this woman in his life. Da'nessa knew in her spirit that she had a soul tie with this man and that she wanted to be part of his life, no matter what the cost.

The flight was twelve hours with one quick stop for refueling in Hawaii, but to both of them, it seemed like the flight was just a few hours. Rupert shared with Da'nessa how his wife Cynthia had put her job before his needs. He confessed to her that Cynthia was self-centered. He shared how he knew that she didn't want children, although she never said it too his face. He admitted to her that day on the plane that his wife was the most selfish person he knew and that his mom had warned him before he married her. Rupert also spoke lovingly about his parents. He told her about his brother, sister-in-law, and their four kids. How much he enjoyed being around them. He told her how his grandfather died the day he was born and that he was named after him. He wanted to tell Da'nessa everything about his life. He wanted her to know him better, and he wanted to get to know her as well.

Da'nessa's listening skills and attention to details really impressed Rupert. She shared with him her plans to go see her great grandma

Bessie as a surprise gift for the eighty-fifth birthday party. She told him that she was her great grandmother's favorite grandchild. Da'nessa shared the family secrets about grandma Bessie's special insight and how she is able to read people without knowing their background. It was a gift that was passed down genetically to Da'nessa.

She shared her life story with him. How she was raised by her aunt and uncle but was not aware of it until she turned ten years old. That she really thought that they were her birth parents. She told him how much she loved them and how they never treated her any different from their own biological kids. She told him about her birth mother and their relationship throughout the years. How their relationship had developed into a sisterhood.

Da'nessa even shared her biggest fear with him. The fear of rejection! She always secretly felt rejected by life situations. She told how God had delivered her from those feelings and helped her to appreciate the small things in life. Small things like being able to sit in a first-class seat on a long flight without paying the price for upgrade. They both burst into laughter. She liked it when he seemed happy; yet, she knew in her heart that he was hurting. Before their flight ended, Rupert asked Da'nessa if they can exchange phone numbers. He was even bold enough to give her his parent's phone number.

By the time they landed in California to make their connecting flights, both had wished the trip would have lasted longer. Da'nessa had thirty minutes to get to her next departing gate. Rupert had an hour and a half. He walked her to her gate and sit with her until she boarded the plane. He wanted so much to hold her in his arms and kiss her long and hard on the lips, but he knew that was wrong and lustful of him. Instead, he embraced her with a warm tight hug and kissed her on the forehead. It was very sweet and tender. A kiss and a moment she will never forget.

Da'nessa's flight to South Georgia was quick. The entire time she thought of nothing but being with Rupert. She prayed for him and all the pain he was experiencing. She prayed for his family. His father, bother, sister-in-law, and kids. She felt as if they were a part of her. She felt even stronger that Rupert was a part of her. He had captured her heart. She knew these feelings were wrong, but her heart longed for him. She wanted to protect him and give him the kind of love she felt he so desired. She thought to herself, why does it seem that women get good men who don't really deserve them? She would have to make a note to herself to ask God that question when she gets home to heaven to be with Him one day.

JOURNAL 5

An Open Door

Ask and it will be given to you;
seek and you will find.

—Matthew 7:7 (KJV)

Rupert's family was not surprised that Cynthia was not with him at the airport, although no one said a word. He explained what happened, and the subject was never discussed again. Cynthia arrived in time for the service. It was a beautiful service, and Rupert saw friends from high school that he had not seen in years.

Yet, he kept thinking about Da'nessa. He hoped she had enjoyed her family. He tried to call her once but got a machine and did not leave a message. He desired to see her face and smell her scent because to him she always smelled fresh, like clean soap. He thought to himself that she is such a beautiful woman inside and out. He missed her. How strange, for the first time since marrying Cynthia, he missed another woman.

Rupert and Cynthia return to Guam, but things were different. Cynthia felt coldness from Rupert that she had never felt before. She knew he was still upset with her for missing the flight. She decided she would give him his space by avoiding him, and she devoted more time to work. Cynthia loved her work. It gave her a sense of control.

She had worked her way up to head operating room nurse. She was important in the hospital, and she loved the respect and feeling that importance afforded her.

Da'nessa was unsure about calling Rupert. He was grieving the loss of his mother. She understood that when people are vulnerable, they do strange things. She didn't call him while she was at home. She was unaware that he had tried to call her at her parent's home. She didn't call him because she was unsure how to handle such communication.

Now that they were back on Guam, he felt close to Da'nessa and wanted to see her. From his office, he picked up the phone and called her dormitory on the naval base. When she was summoned to the phone, he froze for a moment. Finally, he asked how she was doing. They exchanged pleasantries. He wanted to see her. He needed to see her. Not wanting to miss the opportunity, he asked if he could see her. They agreed to meet at the beach in her favorite location on the following day. It was her off day. He was able to get away because his schedule is so flexible. Da'nessa was so nervous. She changed clothing three times. She knew she was meeting a married man, one she can only have conversations with and nothing more, but it still felt like a date.

They met as agreed. Da'nessa had packed a nice snack for them. She had fruit, cheese, crackers, juice, water, and dinner mints. It was a very sweet gesture. Rupert was impressed that she would do such a thing. They lay on the blanket, nibbled on the food, and talked. He told her about the home going service for his mother, and she shared the wonderful news about her great grandmother's party. It was a beautiful outing, but the sun was starting to go down.

Da'nessa knew that it was not wise to be on the beach after dark with a married man, especially one that she had feelings of affections. She began to pack up her things. Rupert started to feel sad because they were about to depart yet again. He reached out and took her by the hand. He held her for what seemed like a long time. He didn't want to let her go. Rupert finally asked if he could kiss her just once. Da'nessa agreed and closed her eyes. When she felt the warmth of his lips and the firmness of his embrace, she melted in his arms. He noticed her lips were soft with a sweet hint of peppermint. How could he release her? He wanted this moment to last forever.

He walked Da'nessa to her car. Then he confessed his true feelings of attachment to her. She too confessed the same feelings. She had tears in her eyes. They both knew that they were wrong. They prayed together silently and asked God to stop them from making this mistake. He is a married man. They had no right to desire one another.

Three weeks passed, and they didn't call or speak to one another. He missed Da'nessa, but he had to be respectable and walk away before they found themselves in the middle of an adulterous affair. It had been tough on her as well. She missed him. Then Da'nessa started to have strange thoughts about him making love to his wife and found that she was jealous. She had to see Cynthia. She wanted to put a face to the name. She knew that Cynthia was a nurse at the naval hospital. Da'nessa decided to go to the hospital just to see her. She needed to make it real somehow, but she had no clue where to start. As the elevator stopped on the fourth floor, a tall elegant African American nurse got on the elevator. Her hair was cut in a flawless "Hallie Berry" style cut, and her nails well-manicured with clear polish.

She was having a conversation with a male doctor concerning a procedure. Da'nessa simply faded into the background until the elevator stopped and the doctor asked Nurse Latimore to finalize the notes and send them to him. The elevator closed, and there the two of them stood. She smiled at Da'nessa, and she smiled in return. Cynthia was all that Da'nessa had imagined and more. She was smart, beautiful, and appeared to be friendly. When they reached her floor, they got off. Cynthia asked if she needed any assistance. Da'nessa said no and walked down the hall toward the stairs.

When Da'nessa reached the stairs, she sat for a moment and cried. She had wanted Cynthia to be a monster, but instead she had appeared to be the total opposite; she was a very nice person. Da'nessa knew what she had to do. The next day at work, she made a huge decision. She submitted a job swap request due to a family hardship. She had to get off the island and away from Rupert. She had heard of others making job swaps for various reasons. Sometimes they are approved and sometimes they were not; those were the words from her job detailer. The detailer is responsible for getting your job assignments in the military.

Da'nessa purposed in her heart to avoid Rupert at all cost. Her feelings were too strong for him, and she didn't trust herself to be near him. Now she felt even more guilty because his wife seems so nice. In Da'nessa's mind, the devil was busy planting thoughts of loneness. She knew she needed to get out and meet other people. Da'nessa's work unit was invited to a Mongolian barbeque by the local island people from their adopted village. Her work unit often participated in volunteer projects with them, such as assisting with home repairs, food and clothing drive, and providing school supplies for the local children. The village was located on the south end of the island. The south end had less rocks but beautiful black-sand beaches. Some say it's due to a underwater volcano system. They are beautiful beaches and well-preserved area. The locals intended to keep it that way.

They will not allow any commercial development in the area. They have only one small retreat accommodation on the small adjacent island inlet called "Cocos Island," and it's a great little getaway. There is limited access to the small island. There are no TVs or phones at the retreat bungalows. The only phone is located in the rental office for emergencies.

It was a Friday night, and Da'nessa had decided prior to rent a bungalow at The Cocos Retreat for the weekend. She needed to get away, and this Mongolian barbeque was a great occasion. Rosemary had worked over the weekend and could not attend with her. The island barbeques were always full of fun, great food and lot of dancing and drinking. She thought to herself, *This is a nice way to relax and get my mind off Rupert.*

As the sun set, the party was in full swing. Everyone was having a great time, including Da'nessa. Some of her coworkers were there, and they all hung out laughing, drinking, and having fun. The weather was beautiful. There was a slight breeze in the air, and the smell of food cooking just added to the delightfulness of this special event. Da'nessa was really just enjoying the festive environment.

Then she noticed him. He had on a white linen summer suit. She could not believe her eyes. Who invited him? She thought about leaving before he spotted her, but for her that would be rude. Why did she feel so guilty? She had not done anything wrong. The last time they met, they shared a simple kiss. Rupert saw Da'nessa sitting and looking beautiful as ever. He went over and spoke to her. She spoke in return to him but seemed a little reserved.

Had he done something wrong? The last time they spoke was on the beach when he asked to kiss her. Why was she treating him this way? Maybe she was there with someone. He didn't understand. He had tried to show her the utmost respect. She had asked him not to communicate after that kiss on the beach. He respected her and wanted to do right by her. Rupert decided to let the matter go. He too was an invited guest, and he wanted to just relax and enjoy himself.

Da'nessa avoided Rupert all evening. He noticed that she was alone but interacted throughout the night with her coworkers. Finally, Rupert was unable to take the coldness of her behavior. He had to know if he had offended her in anyway. He wanted to apologize. She meant too much to him. "Da'nessa, may I speak with you?" he said as he approached her. If he had offended her in any way, he was so sorry. He really didn't understand what was happening and why she was treating him so cold. "Please talk to me," Rupert begged. They decided to go for a walk on the beach. Da'nessa apologized for her cold behavior.

She explained that she was scared of falling in love with him and that if she put up a brick wall, then it wouldn't happen. Rupert pulled Da'nessa close and kissed her hard on the lips. His kiss was so strong, it took her breath away. Rupert looked her in the eyes and told her that he is very much in love with her already, and there is nothing she can do to change the way he felt. He explained that he has not been able to eat or sleep. That she is always on his mind. He told her that he has not made love to his wife since returning from his mother's funeral. Rupert confessed that night after night, he lay in bed thinking about her. How much he wanted to kiss Da'nessa and feel her body next to his. He also confided in her that he feels like a fake in the pulpit because she is always on his mind and not his wife.

Rupert knew he couldn't take being away from her any longer. So he asked Da'nessa to let him make love to her. He said he needed to connect with her in a way that was beyond his framed reference of thinking and knowing. He admitted he had never desire another woman. He confessed that he craved Da'nessa's presence. Rupert knew he was being selfish with this request, but he didn't care anymore. He chose to dishonor his high morals for love. His intentions were not to be disrespectful to God and his grandfather's values. All Rupert could see was his love for Da'nessa at that moment. He knew she was the woman he wanted in his life, and no other would do.

Rupert had to have her, and he was willing to divorce Cynthia. Da'nessa wanted him just as much and agreed to share intimacy with him. In her spirit, she was yelling "no, it's wrong," but her flesh was more than willing to follow her heart. Rupert offered to rent a bungalow, but Da'nessa smiled because she had rented one already for the weekend.

Da'nessa was nervous. She wanted him but was unsure what to do next. Rupert kissed Da'nessa again and again with such passion. Never had she been kissed that way by anyone. Then he slowly undressed her. He was very careful not to rush anything. He wanted to explore her beautiful body. She was well toned with no body fat anywhere. He placed soft kisses on her. Da'nessa could not contain herself. She felt as if she were going to float away on a soft ocean wave. She wanted him and she wanted him badly.

Sensing her excitement, he finished undressing her and placed her on the bed. Then he undressed himself. She was shocked to see his entire physique. She thought to herself with a smile, if she had him in bed every night she would have a truckload of babies by now. Da'nessa asked Rupert to use protection. She wasn't sexually active, but she always kept some standard issued protection in her purse. Rupert agreed and was appreciative that she practices safe sex.

Rupert embraced Da'nessa in his arms as he positioned his body to receive her. He was extremely careful with her because her physique is so much smaller than his. He knew that he was causing her some discomfort as well as pleasure. He asked if she wanted him to stop, but she whispered no as she was enjoying the embrace. They made love for hours. He used her entire box of protection. She lay in his arms late into the night and wondered where do they go from here.

They both knew that they had committed adultery. In her mind, it was the worst kind of adultery because he is a minister. They were expected to live their lives at a higher standard than most people. Which is a great expectation to place on anyone. She reasoned within her mind that we all live in sinful flesh. Rupert had needs, just as well as any other man, and he knew he needed her. Who was she kidding? All sin is sin. There is no big sin and little sin. Wrong or right, she was where she wanted to be.

Da'nessa drifted off to sleep. She awoke to the smell of breakfast. Rupert had gotten breakfast and a few other items from the main island. They spent the entire weekend in bed making love and talking. He did not want this time to end. He felt such a relief. He didn't care that Cynthia would come home and find the house unoccupied. He left her a message on the machine that he will be away for the weekend to think. He was with the woman he loved. He didn't care about what Cynthia was feeling or thinking.

As Da'nessa lay in his arms, he said something she had not expected. Rupert confessed that he wanted to be with her forever and that he was in love with her. He said he loved her ever since the plane trip back home for his mom's funeral. He wants to leave Cynthia, get a divorce, and leave the pulpit. Stop preaching all together.

For the first time, Da'nessa felt fear. She never wanted to break up his marriage. How can she ask God to forgive her for such a sinful act? She knew what the Bible said about "divorce" because her home church had a Bible study series years ago. She also knew she was guilty of winning his heart away from Cynthia. To add insult to injury, how can she be responsible for this man leaving the service of the Lord? He belonged in the pulpit preaching. How did she get here? Her head was spinning. She needed to think.

JOURNAL 6

Slippery Slope

*Remember, too, that knowing what is right to
do and then not doing it is a sin.*

—James 4:17 (NIV)

When Rupert returned home two days later, he found Cynthia upset. She had broken several of his most precious items. She approached him with fire in her eyes. She asked had he been with another woman. He was totally honest and said yes. Her heart hit the floor, and she was crushed. She then asked if he made love to this woman, and again he answered yes. For the first time in their relationship, Cynthia felt real pain and hurt.

She never thought Rupert would do this to her. He is the one man in the world that she knew had a high level of integrity. How could he do this to her? She decided to push the issue, so she asked if he loves the other woman. At first, he refused to answer so he wouldn't hurt her. Cynthia pressed the issue until finally he told her the truth. He said yes. He was in love with someone else.

Cynthia went into their bedroom, closed the door, and cried for the next twelve hours. Rupert gave her some space. He went into the spare bedroom, showered, changed into some gym clothing, and went to play basketball. He knew what he had done was wrong, but there was no taking it back. He missed Da'nessa already and wanted so much to see her. His feelings for Cynthia had faded. He didn't care that she was at home crying.

Cynthia missed work for the next five days, which was a shock to him. She loved her job more than him, so why didn't she return to work? That's her normal escape route. For the first time in her life, she realized that she could lose the only man that ever really loved her. She knew Rupert loved her, and she knew that she had forced him into the arms of another woman. How could she be so stupid, she thought.

Rupert was concerned about Cynthia. He had never seen her this way. She seemed depressed. He couldn't understand why because all she ever wanted was her career. He decided to approach her to discuss the divorce. Maybe then she could move on with her life. In a turn of events, Cynthia begged and cried because she didn't want a divorce. She did not want to lose Rupert. She wanted her marriage. She begged him to go to marriage counseling. She even used scripture on him. She refused to get a divorce. She didn't care that he had a new lover. She didn't want to lose the only person she really loved. For the first time, Rupert was unsure what to do next.

The sin was committed. The damaged was done. Rupert shared everything with Da'nessa that was going on in his marriage. He told Da'nessa that Cynthia didn't want the divorce, but he was willing to take her to court and sue for divorce. He wanted Da'nessa by his side through the divorce process. Da'nessa was so very confused. She loved Rupert very much, but she was dealing with so much guilt. There was no real peace in this situation. Could she and Rupert really have any happiness knowing that their relationship started off so wrong? She was lost. So she did the one thing she knew how to do. She got on her knees, repented again, and prayed. "Father God," she said, "if it is Your will for us to be together, let the job swap fall through. But if it is not Your will, let me get a job swap, and for a very good reason. Then I will know it's according to Your will and divine purpose." Da'nessa believed with all her heart that God would answer her heartfelt prayer.

God always provides a way of escape when it's not His will. Da'nessa was at work on the following Monday when the military job detailer called and said he had a job swap for her. She had one week to decide. If she accepted the swap, they would switch within three weeks. Anything beyond three weeks, the government will not cover the moving expense.

It so happened that the young military lady needing the swap was a native of Guam. She needed to return home to care for her sick mother. She had prayed and applied for the swap on faith and was so thankful it had become available. The young sailor's mother was dying of cancer, and she needed to be home with her.

Da'nessa remembered her prayer and accepted the swap. She knew she had to leave the island. Her next work duty station would be Orlando, Florida, near her family. She did not want to break up Rupert's marriage. She would always judge herself for doing so. She was not an adulterer, and she was not going to live the life of adultery. In addition to that, she refused to be the reason Rupert gave up ministering. It was his birthright, and they both knew it.

JOURNAL 7

New Start, But Old Habits

Flee sexual immorality.
Every sin that a man does is outside the body,
but he who commits sexual immorality sins against his own body.

—1 Corinthians 6:18 (NKJV)

Da'nessa arrived in sunny Orlando, Florida. She had heard of the tourism industry that dominated the Orlando market area of the state. It was so different from the laid-back lifestyle on Guam. Yet, the naval base seemed miles away from all the hoopla. Which was a mixed blessing. It was important to her to adjust to life in her new location.

Da'nessa always located a really good church as part of her adjustment process. She had prayed, repented, and asked God to forgive her and Rupert. Her heart was good and kind. She loved Jesus and God. Her desire was to do as right as possible.

Her departure from Rupert had been bittersweet. She had asked him to stay with his wife and to release her heart. Da'nessa felt that she had no right to be happy with Rupert because their relationship had started wrong. She knew in her heart that she would always love him. They both cried in each other's arms her entire last night on the island.

He had a big hole in his heart. He knew he had to let go. It was very painful to do so. He asked Da'nessa to write to him, but she refused. They had to make a clean break. They had to trust God to keep their hearts and souls during this difficult time. This decision killed her inside, but she quickly learned to suppress her emotions.

Da'nessa's transition into her new routine of life in Orlando was slow and lonely. After about six months, she met a nice single young man named Trevor and started to date again. He was no Rupert. He was polar opposite. Trevor was a serious person, and he rarely smiled. He had a kind and respectable demeanor. Da'nessa went through the motion of dating, but no real sparks. He was good company but nothing more. Something appeared to be missing in their relationship. There was no real connection. Just a few dates and some small talk on the phone a few nights a week. Da'nessa had no intentions of getting close to Trevor. Sadly, he was just a space filler for boredom, nothing more.

She had a soul tie to Rupert and found herself comparing Trevor to him. Trevor did not attend church regularly. He had been raised in the church but found that he didn't trust people in the church. Trevor harbored a very darker secret. He had been molested as a child by a pastor in his local church. He never told anyone about his tainted past until he met Da'nessa. All those years, he felt no one would believe him. He held it in for such a long time until the final result was him becoming a bitter young man. According to Trevor, he stopped going to church when he was old enough to decide. Da'nessa never asked him to attend church service with her. Her thinking was if he didn't want to go to church, then don't go. Faith is an individual experience. Everyone of age has a choice. She went to church faithfully. She explored several churches before settling on this one particular Baptist church.

It is a small church, similar to her church back home, except her home church was Methodist. The pastor of this church is an attractive man named Pastor Vernon Kennedy. He is tall and on the slim side. He appears to be in his early fifties. He has charisma, and his sermons are very powerful. He could easily pastor a megachurch if he chose to.

The first lady of the church, his wife, on the other hand, is a small, shy, timid woman who seems withdrawn. Her name is Donna Kennedy. She is a nice person, but she seems to have no real friends. First Lady Donna is an only child. Her dad is a well-known pastor from New Orleans, LA. First Lady had been raised in a very sheltered environment. Her mom passed away when she was thirteen years old. Her dad sent her off to an all-girl boarding school in New England. By her senior year, her father had remarried. It was rumored that she did not like her stepmother, and they did not get along. Her stepmother was considered a loose woman who brought shame to the family name.

Yet, First Lady Donna's father stayed with her stepmother until he passed away. After his death, her stepmother took all of the family possessions. She claimed there was no legal will. First Lady Donna accepted life for what it was: a series of misfortunate events. Nothing seems to faze her. Maybe she had learned not to trust church people also.

Da'nessa had been attending this church off and on for the past six months. She had considered joining, but there was always something in the back of her mind nagging at her. Maybe it was the fact that it was a Baptist church and not Methodist.

One Sunday, Trevor asked to attend church with her. She thought it was great ideal and welcomed him. Maybe he was ready to release his pain from the past. She had felt that they were unequally yoked because he didn't attend church. There was no way she wanted a man outside of the church for a lifelong partner. They arrived at church prior to praise and worship. Da'nessa always believes in arriving early. Trevor seems okay but was really quiet and unmoved through the entire service. He seemed to be distracted, she thought. Was it that painful for him to return to the House of God? Something was really making Trevor unsettled. Da'nessa decided not to let his behavior bother her.

The drive home from church was interesting. Out of the blue, Trevor asked Da'nessa if Pastor Kennedy had flirted with her. She was shocked by such a question. She told him no, but Trevor insisted the pastor was watching them the entire service. Da'nessa disagreed and explained that it's the speaker's job to connect with his audience. He was most likely watching everyone.

Trevor insisted something about Pastor Kennedy is not right. To her, Trevor was just being paranoid. He had shared part of his childhood experience concerning pastors with her, so she concluded that he was really overacting. Da'nessa continued to go to the church despite Trevor's reservation. She loved the church choir because they always sing up-to-date songs that young people can relate to. Da'nessa also felt that Pastor Kennedy gave very good sermons each Sunday. His sermons always seem to confirm what she had read in the Bible during the week. She seems to really connect spiritually. Nothing was out of the ordinary, until one Sunday about six weeks after Trevor had attended service.

Da'nessa was in church service, and it was almost over. She had an airplane flight to catch. It was a training detail for two weeks with her job. The pastor was just about to conduct altar call, to invite people to join the church as members, when she decided to leave out of service. By the time she reached her car, a voice asked if she was in a rush to leave so soon. She knew that voice because she had heard it so many times before. When Da'nessa turned to face the voice, it was that of Pastor Kennedy. *How did he get out here so quick?* she thought to herself. He was in the pulpit about to do altar call.

Pastor Kennedy approached her and extended his hand to say hello. Da'nessa in return said hello and introduced herself. She explained that she had a flight to catch and said goodbye. Two Sundays later, she returned to church. The church had a guest speaker that day, but the pastor was in attendance. It was the Pastor's tenth anniversary of pastoring that church. The church had a large crowd in attendance. Near the end of service, Da'nessa decided to leave early to avoid the rush of everyone leaving the parking lot at the same time.

By the time Da'nessa reached her car, Pastor Kennedy approached her again? "Do you have another flight?" he asked with a slight grin on his face.

"No," she explained. "I'm just trying to beat the crowd. Shouldn't you be in the pulpit attending your flock?" Da'nessa asked.

"I'm more concerned with the one trying to get away," he said.

She was flattered by his comment. He extended his hand to open her car door and then asked her to please attend again. Da'nessa thought it strange that he would go to such lengths and wondered if he was this way with all new non-members. Da'nessa returned to church every Sunday, and most of the time, Pastor Kennedy would be in the parking lot to say a few words to her as she departed. She found herself looking forward to the attention. There was some-thing about him she liked. Maybe in a small way, he reminded her of Rupert. She often wondered about Rupert. Rosemary had written and told her that he and his wife had twin boys, Rosemary said it had been announced in church. It appeared that Rupert had moved on with his life.

Cynthia had blessed him with what he craved the most. He had twin boys, his heir and a spare. He had everything he wanted, and now surely he is happy with his little family. So Da'nessa thought! She was sure he had not even given her another thought. She rea-soned within her mind that here she was in sunny Orlando, Florida, enjoying the attention of yet another married man. Not just any mar-ried man but a married ministered. Da'nessa was on a slippery slope. She knew in her heart of hearts that it was wrong to desire Pastor Kennedy's affections. Da'nessa wanted to believe that he was just a friendly man, but in the back of her mind, she knew better. She was a very bright young lady who had wisdom beyond her young tender years. She knew their little meeting game was leading to something more serious.

It was the first Sunday in August, which happens to be her birthday. As always, Pastor Kennedy intercepted her in the park-ing lot after service. She told him that it was her birthday. He said "happy birthday" and open her door for her. The following Sunday, as Da'nessa left service and approached her car, there was a small gift box wrapped in pretty paper taped to her windshield. The note inside read: "Something special for someone so special and a phone number."

It was a beautiful charm bracelet from Kay Jewelers. It looked expensive. Da'nessa took the bracelet to the mall at Kay's Jewelers and was shown a similar one. It was an expensive gift. She knew who it was from and decided to call and say thank you. Da'nessa called the phone number on the card. She knew it was Pastor Kennedy's number. As it turned out, it was the private number to his office at the church.

JOURNAL 8

The Substitute Solution

When Pride comes, then come shame;
But with the humble is wisdom.

—Proverbs 11:2 (NKJV)

Da'nessa and Pastor Kennedy talked on the phone several times a week. She loved talking to him. He was smart and funny. He never made a romantic move; he just seemed to want a friend. All of this communication was making her develop feelings for him. She enjoyed seeing him in church. It was their private game. He would buy her gifts of clothing items, and she would wear them. Some were not the sort of gifts a young girl should accept from any man, and especially a married pastor. They were not the sort that a pastor should be purchasing.

This was wrong on so many levels, but Da'nessa was having too much fun to let go. She had somehow convinced herself that it was okay because they were not having sex. It was just a friendly game of companionship with limits. One day, he asked if she wanted to take a trip, all-expense paid. Da'nessa loved his gifts and was happy to accept more.

Da'nessa's countenance changed after hearing about Rupert and Cynthia's babies. Something inside of her was hurting and jealous.

She didn't want to hurt; she wanted to forget. She was also starting to forget her strict Christian walk. She appeared to be mad at God, the church, Rupert, and herself. But she hid it well. She kept attending church, but her heart was not committed anymore. She was physically in church every Sunday and Wednesday, but church was not in her spiritually.

Pastor Kennedy was to be the guest pastor at a large well-known church in Tampa, Florida. He asked Da'nessa to meet him in Tampa. He told her what hotel and asked her to arrive one day prior to him. They could not be seen together publicly. He was well-connected in Tampa, so she understood his concern. He arranged to have her room connected to his but under a separate account. He gave her a private credit card for the expenses and a certified letter, if questioned. The room was in her name, but he paid for everything.

It was only a two-hour drive from her home in Orlando. The hotel was beautiful, and the room had been set up with flowers and candy. There was also a gift waiting for her at the hotel concierge desk with a noted that read "see you at nine in the morning." She had all day to herself. She asked about a local spa and hair salon. She pampered herself at Pastor Kennedy's expense. By nine o'clock, she was excited. Da'nessa looked beautiful in her lovely lingerie gift. The gift was a sexy teal blue lingerie. It was made of fine silk and very soft to the touch. He had picked out the correct size, and it really fit her beautiful body. The silk lay on every curve of her firm body. There was no doubt in her mind what was about to happen, and inside she was ready to give him her all.

It was about nine-twenty in the morning when her room phone rang. The male voice on the other end of the receiver said "open the side door." Then there was a tap on the inside connecting room doors. She knew it was Pastor Kennedy. He entered the room and was pleased to see her standing their desiring him. He reached out and pulled her close. He kissed her on the lips. She wanted so much to be held and made love too. She had dumped Trevor almost a year prior and had not made love to anyone. Da'nessa knew that she was behaving badly, but she really didn't care. Her heart had been broken when she left Guam and Rupert behind.

Da'nessa had determined in her mind that life is not fair. "You try to live right, and all you get is a broken heart," she surmised in her thoughts. Why did God allow her and Rupert to love so deeply? He had reached the very depths of her soul. She would never love that way again. As she made love to Pastor Kennedy, he asked her to call him by his first name, Vernon. She told him everything he wanted to hear, even if it was a lie. They made love throughout the two days of that weekend. Vernon said he had not felt that way in a very long time. The only problem is that they didn't use protection. She knew better but just didn't care. She seem to be self-loathing.

After the trip to Tampa, Vernon and Da'nessa would meet often and make love. He appeared to be enjoying her company. He told her that he had a vasectomy years ago and was unable to have children. She knew in her heart that she was faking their lovemaking. She just didn't seem to give a darn anymore. He was spoiling her with beautiful gifts, and all she had to do was help him relieve some stress by using her body. She had no intentions of being anything beyond his lover.

Da'nessa and Vernon got careless. It was early on a Wednesday morning about five-thirty. She met Pastor Kennedy at his office. It was something they did from time to time. She would always park her car two blocks away from his office. The encounter was always quick. Just a little rendezvous before work, and he in return would provide her with precious gifts. He loved giving her things. She seemed so excited like a child at Christmas. It made him feel like a man. He was able to provide for her. He knew she was a woman with a career, but his salary could afford her luxury; she could not buy for herself. This thought alone made him stand tall with his chest poked out as he watched her beam with excitement every time. He was the older man with this young beautiful woman desiring him as much as he desired her.

This Wednesday morning, they made love in Pastor Kennedy's office. His back was to the door, but the door was not locked. In the middle of all their passion, they had forgotten to lock the door. Being so into their activities that morning, they had not notice the door eased open. It was his wife, First Lady Donna Kennedy.

In her meek way of doing things, she said good morning to them as if they had just sat down to breakfast. He stopped making love and turned toward her. She handed him a towel. She looked at Da'nessa and asked her to get dressed and leave. His wife didn't make a fuss at all. She somehow seems detached from reality. She operated like a robot. She was cold and unfeeling. Maybe the hurt from her dad marrying a tart had taught her not to care.

Da'nessa felt so ashamed. As she dressed, his wife began to speak. "Please don't think you are so special," she said. "He has done this on more than one occasion. I know he spends money on you and treats you like a queen." Her words shocked Da'nessa. First Lady continued to speak, "This is how he vents. I'm not mad at you because I know he pursued you. He always pursues them. I let him have his fun, but when he starts to get careless, then I put a stop to it."

First Lady Kennedy asked Da'nessa to never return to their church again. She said to her, "Being a first lady is tough, and I pray you never have to experience it." "Some of us learn to look the other way. Trusting God will take the revenge." There was such a coldness in her voice. "Now leave," she said, "he won't need your services any longer. We always change the phone number to his private study. If you try to continue to see him, it will get ugly."

Pastor Kennedy was in his private study taking a shower. He never came out to say goodbye or plead with her not to go. Da'nessa knew then that everything his wife said was the truth. She had a new level of respect for First Lady Kennedy, more than she had for herself. Yet, Da'nessa also felt very sorry for her. She knew that First Lady Kennedy was living her life in a cage. Why would she stay with such a man and in such a situation?

A valuable lesson was learned that day. Da'nessa learned that with much power comes much responsibility. When you live your life in public as a woman of God, you must act with grace. She also learned that some powerful men lie and that they don't always treat their women well. Da'nessa did leave their church, and she never returned. She did it out of self-respect, but mostly for his wife. There was no real loss for her. She had promised herself that no one will ever hurt her heart again. Nothing could ever hurt as worse as losing Rupert.

JOURNAL 9

No More Shame

The righteous cry out, and the Lord hears, and
delivers them out of all their troubles.

—Psalm 34:17 (NKJV)

Da'nessa found a new church to attend. This one was a megachurch. She felt for sure that nothing could happen here. A church this big, there is no way the pastor can know everyone, so surely she would not be a temptation anymore. Da'nessa would purposely sit in the back of the church. It was a large church with about five thousand members. It was a solid church with a strong deacon board. Deacon board is a group of married men that governs the church business along with the pastor.

She felt safe here from her sinful adultery side of her personality. She quickly fell into the routine of things. Each Sunday, she would attend Sunday school at 9:00 a.m. and church service at 10:30 a.m. Often, when time permitted, she would attend Wednesday night Bible study. Da'nessa never thought she would enjoy attending such a large church. She was sure it would be cold and unfriendly. Yet, she felt safe here, and she wanted to be in fellowship with other Christians. She wanted to be near people who loved God, hoping the encounters would safely turn her heart back to God.

Da'nessa discovered that large churches tend to have core groups that operate like minifamilies. Whatever ministry you volunteered and worked with, that's where your bond is formed. After about one year of attending church service, she decided to do some volunteering at the church. She joined the youth ministry staff.

It was a well-organized machine that served about two hundred children each Sunday, except second Sunday. Second Sunday is always devoted to youth day at the church, so all the children met in the main sanctuary for service. The youth department also held Vacation Bible School each summer, along with youth rallies, concerts, and a Puppet Ministry.

Da'nessa was fascinated by the Puppet Ministry and decided to become a volunteer/puppeteer. This ministry had ten children ranging from ages ten to sixteen years of age. It was run by a friendly couple, Reverends James and Peggy Grant, who were associate ministers of the church. The group practiced on the second and fourth Saturday each month and mostly performed on fourth Sundays for the children.

The Puppet Ministry was so much fun. It was great to watch the kids learn about Christ through this ministry. The children were so excited by the movement of the puppets. Everything appeared to be going very well. Da'nessa felt that she had finally found her ministry where she was to serve God. It's funny how life always throws you a curve ball.

It was Wednesday afternoon when the phone rang. The caller ID displayed the church name. Da'nessa thought it was strange because she rarely got calls from the church. She answered the phone. On the other end of the line was Minister Peggy Grant. She was one of the associate ministers over the youth ministry. *Have I forgotten a meeting or something,* thought Da'nessa? She answered the phone, and Minister Peggy asked to speak with Da'nessa. Then she said to her, "Are you planning to attend Bible study tonight?"

"If you are, can we meet for a few minutes prior to service?" Da'nessa agreed that they would meet at 5:30 p.m. in the Youth Ministry Office. Da'nessa arrived about 5:15 p.m. She is always one to arrive early. It was just her way of doing things. When they met, Minister Peggy looked as if she had been crying. At first, Da'nessa thought something had happened to one of the children on the

Puppet Ministry. The environment seemed so gloomy. "Is everything okay?" she finally asked Minister Peggy.

Minister Peggy stopped crying and pulled herself together. She apologized for her behavior. She then explained to Da'nessa that she will be resigning from the ministry and leaving the church. Da'nessa was shocked. She could not make herself inquire as to why she was resigning. She did manage to ask if everything was okay. Maybe it was health-related; she knew that Minister Peggy had overcome cancer and was a ten-year survivor.

Minister Peggy was very open with Da'nessa. She told her that she and her husband Minister James Grant were getting a divorce. They had been married thirty-five years. They were high school sweethearts. They had no children because she was unable to have them. They thought about adoptions but decided instead to just work with the youth ministry.

She also informed Da'nessa that her husband had left the church with a younger woman and that he and the young lady were expecting a baby. The young lady in question is only twenty-seven years old. The shame of this scandal is too much for Minister Peggy to bear. Although she loved living in Orlando, Florida, she was returning home to her family in Michigan. They will be a strong support for her during this difficult time.

This breaking news deeply affected Da'nessa. She knew firsthand about adultery. She had worked hard over the past two years to avoid that sin. Da'nessa was unaware that the couple was having marital problems. Her heart wept for her. She could feel her pain. With both of them leaving the church, the puppet ministry had no leader. Minister Peggy asked Da'nessa to be in charge of the puppet ministry only. She told her that she knew how much she loved the ministry. She had no doubt she would do a great job.

Minister Peggy had also asked to recommend her name to the church bishop as the replacement, along with the others who were to assume different positions on the youth ministry team. Da'nessa had a knot in her stomach. This was a big responsibility. Minister Peggy sensed her apprehension and told her it was okay. She did recommend keeping the puppet ministry small and local. They should only perform at youth church on fourth Sunday. She did not want the ministry to fall apart because it is such a wonderful learning tool for the children. The request is only a temporary fix until they select a new youth ministry director to run the department. Da'nessa agreed and accepted the task.

Over the next six months, the ministry ran smooth. It is a good ministry, and Da'nessa stayed true to the request, and they only performed mostly at their church youth events. Da'nessa loved the children who were puppeteers, and they loved her. She had no children of her own so she spoiled them with treats, skate parties, and sporting events. Life was going well and drama-free until Easter season the following year. The Puppet Ministry decided to put on a large Easter production the Saturday before Easter Sunday. The production had special effects, such as fog, special lighting, music, and much fanfare.

It was a beautiful production that gave great honor to the children on the puppet team and their parents. The event was even videoed for future viewing. When the program was over, closing remarks were normally conducted by Da'nessa or the new director of Youth Ministry Pastor Tammy McGee. To everyone's surprise, the bishop of the church was in attendance at this event and came forward to give the closing remarks. His name is Bishop Craig Reed. He is the head pastor of New Freedom Missionary Baptist Church. It was rare to see the bishop out at such a small event. He had apparently brought his two grandkids to see the program. He was so impressed with the production that he had to comment. Bishop Reed went on stage and announced to all he was overjoyed with the performance. He called Da'nessa and the other puppeteers up to the stage to personally thank them for doing such a wonderful job with the children's ministry.

Bishop Reed held Da'nessa's hand as he spoke kindly of all that she and the team had accomplished. Da'nessa was grateful but felt a little strange on the inside. She felt as if he was pulling her close to him as he gave his warm remarks. Da'nessa was too embarrassed to release his hand because she did not want to appear rude. The night was filled with excitement. The show was finally over, and everyone was ready to go home. The team completed their routine cleanup procedures and had the closing prayer.

JOURNAL 10

Not This Time

*Blessed is the man who endures temptation: for when he
has been approved, he will receive the crown of life which
the Lord has promised to those who love Him.*

—James 1:12 (NKJV)

The next day in church service, the bishop once again mentioned the puppet ministry event and asked all involved to stand. Then they showed on the overhead projection a brief clipping from the production. It was very impressive, to say the least. Da'nessa was proud but also embarrassed to be called out so publicly. Her one desire at this church was to remain in the background. Fate had dealt her a new hand.

About two weeks passed when she received a phone call from the church. It was the church secretary. She asked if Da'nessa could come in for a meeting with the bishop. Da'nessa was shocked to say the least. She wanted to inquire about the nature of the meeting but was too scared to say anything. She agreed to a meeting.

She didn't know what to wear to meet the bishop, so she decided to dress as if she were going to an interview. She wore one of her best blue business suit. It was a nice A-line skirt with a short jacket. It was very well made and fit her body nicely. She also wore three-inch black high-heel pumps. She dared not cross her legs, otherwise someone might notice the red bottom on her heels. She wasn't vain; she just loved those shoes. Was she overdressed? She thought to herself. Anyone who knew women shoes knew that red bottoms were expensive shoes. To her, they were just her lucky shoes.

Da'nessa prayed and asked God not to let this outfit be vanity on her part. Her only desire was to be professional. At least that's what she told herself. Da'nessa was early for the appointment. She always arrived early. It was the way she was taught to do things. Why the bishop had sent for her, she wondered, still not knowing the reason for the meeting.

The bishop's office is beautiful. Everything was in its perfect place. She was asked to sit at a small table near the window. The view was awesome. It overlooked a large pond with a waterfall that sprayed multicolor water. How strange, she had never known there was a pond on the other side of the church. It was a well-kept secret.

Da'nessa was most impressed with the bishop's book collection. She loved books, especially really old ones with beautiful binding. He had various pictures of his family throughout the office. You could tell he was a family man. The bishop and his secretary joined Da'nessa at the table. She was offered water, juice, coffee, or tea. She chose a cup of coffee.

The bishop started the meeting with a prayer. Then he proceeded to explain why he had called her in the office. He had hoped to offer her some additional funds to increase the Puppet Ministry. The bishop said he felt that the ministry was very beneficial to the children and an excellent learning tool. Da'nessa knew that they could use the money to buy new puppets, props, and a better portable stage. The bishop was thinking on a larger scale than Da'nessa. He wanted her and some of the kids to attend the yearly Baptist conference to learn additional skills. His goal was to take the church puppet ministry outside the church. He intended to offer their services to other churches, and who knows maybe one day have them perform at the national conference as well. That would really make the church stand out amongst the other churches in the area.

All of this was overwhelming to Da'nessa. She was totally impressed but had no desire to increase the ministry. Sensing it was a bit much, the bishop asked her to give it some thought, and if she was up to the challenge, then prepare a proposal within two weeks. His secretary recorded all the details of the meeting. She also asked Da'nessa if she had access to an e-mail account. She would forward her a template of the standard proposal package used by other ministries within the church to complete and submit. The meeting lasted about forty minutes. The bishop walked her to the door. He thanked her for coming, and once again, he held her hand for what seemed like longer than normal.

Da'nessa sat in her car unable to move. She was still overwhelmed from the meeting. She told herself that all she wanted was to attend church and fade in the background. Why was God allowing this to happen to her? God knows her better than anyone at this church. She is a recluse, but worse than that, she is sinner and a danger to married men, especially those in ministry. She was grateful when the new youth pastor turned out to be a woman. She liked Minister Tammy McGee and found her to be very organized. Why didn't the bishop include her in this meeting? She thought to herself. Oh well, it's his church, and he can do what he pleases. Besides, did she really just sense an attraction between herself and the bishop of this large establishment? This cannot be happening again.

Da'nessa wondered if she was a bait that the devil constantly planted in the church to attempt to bring down the man of God. Could she be a wolf in sheep's clothing and not even be aware of it herself? There is something that attracts them to her. What was it? She herself admitted she is no raving beauty. Truthfully, she had a unique plainness about her. Nope, she is just a human living in corruptible flesh. There is nothing special there. Da'nessa knew she had a beautiful spirit. Maybe she is jumping to conclusion on this one. After all, Bishop as done nothing out of the ordinary except hold her hand a minute or two longer than she thought he should have. Da'nessa felt that maybe she is being paranoid. She decided to write the proposal for the puppet ministry funding. She sought the assistance of several people because she wanted the wording to be just right. It was an impressive document. Well-thought-out with all the important figures and details. The budget committee agreed to the funding of her submitted proposal.

The Puppet Ministry was now an official subministry on the church books, and she was its director. Ministries with a budget came with more responsibilities. Da'nessa had to attend meetings for ministry directors; she had to attend continuing education training. She was also asked to attend this year's Baptist Conference in Dallas, Texas.

All the arrangements for the conference were made by the church staff, including the booking of the flights. Da'nessa was to share a room with Lisa Davis, another female minister that was over the women's ministry. The two ladies seem to get along well. Lisa was an older lady and had attended many conferences. She had shared her wisdom with Da'nessa concerning how to behave while attending a conference. Although the conference was in a different state, eyes were always watching. Often, news, in the form of gossip, got back to the church before the conference was over. Da'nessa listened carefully and took heed to the advice.

The conference lasted six days. It started on a Sunday with the opening sermon around 5:00 p.m. local time. There were various workshops and different sermons throughout the week. Da'nessa had registered for the Puppet Ministry Training and New Youth Focus workshop. Both offered the newest ideals on the market. The nightly sermons were also inspirational. Bishop Reed was set to speak on Friday night of the conference. He didn't arrive in Dallas until Friday morning. His secretary had arranged a debriefing luncheon for all of his staff members. There were twelve members there, but only eleven attended the luncheon on Friday morning. Lisa Davis received an emergency call from home and had to fly back to Orlando.

The luncheon was a very nice gathering. It was refreshing to hear the various reports of new materials, including some from the Puppet Ministry. Everyone returned to their rooms to rest before gathering again when the bishop was set to speak at the main conference that night. An hour after returning to her room, the phone rang. It startled Da'nessa, and she almost didn't answer. On the other end of the phone was a voice she was sure she recognized. As it turned out, it was Bishop Reed. Da'nessa froze stiff, not sure how to respond. Bishop made small talk at first, but then he asked her a serious question. He asked if she would join him later for a late-night private dinner. He said it would be exclusive and that he would arrange for a driver to pick her up around 10:00 p.m. Da'nessa no longer had any doubts about his intentions.

She was crushed. She had so much respect for him. How could she have been so wrong? She knew the signs and had picked up on them early on. She should have walked away after that fateful night of the Easter production. Why was this happening again? She knew that she had to refuse his offer. So she lied and told him that she had plans already to meet some of her classmates from high school who live locally. He expressed how disappointed he was. He asked if she could somehow reschedule with them.

Da'nessa knew that she had to be strong. Maybe this was a test from God to see if He could trust her. Da'nessa was determined not to let God down again. At least not in this area. She had prayed for a breakthrough and this was her chance to prove that she could walk in wisdom. She remembered her talk with Lisa at the beginning of the week. Adultery is wrong, and she knew she was a better person. Da'nessa stood her ground and declined the dinner offer. Bishop Reed sensed that he had chosen the wrong person to invite. He apologized and asked her if she would not mention it to anyone: it was just a friendly dinner invite.

Da'nessa said goodbye and packed her suitcase. She didn't even want to hear his sermon that evening. Which is sad because she loved to hear him speak and always felt that his message was a word from God. Upon return to Orlando, Da'nessa handed in her resignation and left the church for good, never to return. Not even for a visit. Da'nessa was losing faith in the church and decided not to attend any establishments for a while. She continued to pray daily, read her Bible, and often watch church service on television.

JOURNAL 11

Deception in An Unlikely Place

Obey God because you are His children;
don't slip back into your old ways.

—1 Peter 1:14 (TLB, Paraphrased)

It had been about three years, and Da'nessa still had not returned to church on a regular basis. Sometimes when visiting family back home in South Georgia, she would attend her home church, but nothing regularly. She didn't trust herself anymore. She knew that there was an invisible evil force hanging over her that was out to seek and destroy the men serving God.

Da'nessa had prayed for deliverance prior but was too scared to test her faith. She had been reassigned from Orlando, Florida, to Groton, Connecticut. She served at the Groton Navy Dental Center. After twelve years of military service and the threat of Operation Desert Storm War in the air, Da'nessa decided to end her military career. She had gotten out of the navy on an honorable discharge and was now working in the local school system and part-time for the state of Connecticut.

Da'nessa had a good life in Connecticut. In addition to working in the school system, she also worked part-time for the state of Connecticut as a child advocate. She loved debating any program that would better the lives of children. Da'nessa dated off and on but never anyone serious. Until she met him, Michael Joseph. Michael is a social worker for the state of Connecticut. He is a tall and handsome man. They connected as friends immediately and seemed to have a real connection with one another. There was only one problem: Michael is Caucasian and Da'nessa is African American. Mixed couples are nothing unusual in this region. It's just that neither of them had ever dated outside of their race.

At first, they kept their relationship on a professional and friendly level. The two would share an occasional lunch together or talk over the phone. By this time, Da'nessa lived in New London, Connecticut, and Michael had a place in Hartford, Connecticut. It was about an hour drive between the two of them.

One day, Michael invited her to his place for dinner and a movie. He had a nice condo but didn't have much furniture. She didn't give it much thought because some people like things at a minimum. He was the perfect gentleman. He even offered her a key to the condo if she wanted to stay the night and not make the hour drive back home to New London. Michael really cared about her, and he respected her. They had been seeing one another periodically for about six months. He had even driven down to New London to her home. Her place is a small two-bedroom cottage within walking distance of the beach. She had converted one of the bedrooms into a home office/library. The back porch was facing the direction of the beach, and you could hear the sounds of the ocean. It was perfect for her; it reminded her of Guam. A memory she would never forget.

The first time Michael and Da'nessa made love was on a snowy winter night in December. It had been lite snow, off and on all day while she was in Hartford. She had phoned Michael to see how things were going. She told him she was in Hartford and wanted to take him up on his offer to stay over. She also told him that she didn't mind sleeping on the sofa. Michael said it was okay and told her where he secretly kept the spare key, since she declined one of her own.

The condo was nice and warm when she arrived. She knew her way around in the kitchen, so Da'nessa made herself a cup of coffee.

It was a quiet evening, and Michael was not at home. Da'nessa took a shower and found one of his large T-shirts and slipped it on. It was kind of strange to her that Michael didn't have that many clothing in his closet. Then again, she told herself that everyone is different. Besides, he was always handsomely dressed when he was around her. Around 9:30 p.m., the snow was coming down hard outside. Da'nessa watched from the patio window that faced a gated backyard. It was beautiful and peaceful. The snow has a way of making outside seem lighter from the reflection. Although it was after 9:00 p.m., it seemed much earlier.

Da'nessa heard a strange noise, as if the garage door had opened. She was not expecting Michael because he had gone to Middletown, Connecticut, on personal business. A minute later, Michael walked into the room. "Hi, you," she said. "This is a nice surprise." Michael had a big smile on his face. "You are a nice surprise, especially standing there in nothing but my T-shirt," he said. All she could do was blush. He gave her a big hug and embraced her for a good long minute. She asked if he wanted something to eat, but he said no. So she made him some hot chocolate. She knew he loved hot chocolate. Michael told her was going to jump in the shower. He promised to be back in a few minutes.

Michael is a good guy. She didn't know why she felt the need to hide their relationship. He never seems to press the issue, so she did not either. They were both happy with their little arrangement. When Michael got out of the shower, he joined her in front of the patio door. He sipped his hot chocolate while looking out the window. Michael was only wearing a towel around his waist. He put down his beverage. Took Da'nessa in his arms and kissed her for a very long time. There they stood in front of the snowy view. Finally, he released her and closed the blinds. He had wanted to make love to her for a very long time.

Michael was very gentle in his lovemaking. He explored every inch of her body as if he were committing it to memory. He loved her mocha-color skin. It was soft all over and very firm to the touch. He knew she worked out several times a week, and it showed. Every part of her body was well-defined like a weight lifter but still soft to the touch. He kissed her repeatedly. As he lay on the floor, Da'nessa caressed his body in her warm hands and gave him a body massage. Michael could not contain himself any longer. They made passionate love. He was gentle with her because he felt the tension and knew in his mind that she had not been with a man in a long time. He was amazed. They enjoyed being with one another. Yet, thankful that the protection he was wearing stayed put. They made love several more times before drifting off to sleep.

The next morning when Da'nessa woke up, Michael had left already but left her a warm note of thanks for a lovely night. She lay quietly in his comfortable king-size bed. She could tell that the lining was expensive. He seems to have expensive taste anyway. Da'nessa's clothing was clean and folded neatly on the lovely chase in the bedroom. Michael had laundered them for her. He is such a thoughtful man, she thought to herself. She lay there for another two hours waiting to ensure the roads had safely been plowed before she made her attempt to return home to New London. She showered, got dressed, and sealed the note with a big kiss of red lipstick.

It was another two months before the lovers got together again. Michael had invited Da'nessa to join him in Las Vegas, Nevada. He had prearranged everything, including her limo to the airport. When Da'nessa arrived at the Luxor Hotel in Las Vegas, she was totally impressed by the first-class service. Michael had taken care of everything. He had found the time to shop for her as well. How did he know her clothing size and style? she wondered. She thought back on the day they made love, and he had laundered her clothing. At this point, who really cares? She was just enjoying the moment. It seems like a dream come true. Like all dreams, sooner or later, you wake up to a nightmare. Paradise was not going to last.

They had been in Vegas for two wonderful days. It was the last night of their little minivacation. Michael decided to take Da'nessa to a beautiful restaurant for dinner and show. Everything was great until they were leaving the event. How could everything go wrong so fast? Michael was standing, holding Da'nessa's hand waiting for their limo to arrive. Two elderly women approached them. "Hello, Pastor Joseph," was their greeting to him. "You are Pastor Joseph from Middletown, Connecticut," replied one of the ladies. Michael looked stunned and did not respond. At that time, the limo arrived, and he helped Da'nessa into the car. Da'nessa was confused and demanded an explanation. Michael was at a loss for words. How could he explain to her that he had been living a double life and been so dishonest?

Not sure what to say, he asked her to give him time to think. He got out the Limo. He wanted to walk and think about how to discuss this dilemma. He closed the limo door and asked the driver to take Da'nessa back to the Luxor Hotel. Michael returned to the hotel late that night. Da'nessa was upset. Why didn't he tell her he was a pastor? She was hurt and disappointed. She told Michael she could never trust him again. She closed the bedroom door, and he slept on the couch. Da'nessa left early without waking him.

Danessa flew back to Connecticut alone and in shock. The flight was long and cold. She could not believe what had happened. She had no idea he was a pastor. Now she wondered if he was married. How could she not have known? He was so kind to her, why didn't he tell her the truth up-front? They had shared so much. Yet, she too had not revealed all of her past. She had been too ashamed to tell him everything. It's amazing how the truth can catch up with you.

When the plane landed, the limo service was there to meet her and take her home to New London. It was a wet rainy day, which didn't matter to her because it was raining in her heart as well. Da'nessa cried for three days. She did not hear from Michael, and his phone number was disconnected. To her, all the signs were those of a married man. Dear God, how could she have gotten involved with another married pastor? Da'nessa was starting to believe her life was truly cursed. She had pain inside because she had opened her heart to this man. She had feelings for him. Feelings she had only felt for one other man. Was this lifestyle just happening to her, or were there other women out there who experienced the same thing? Maybe there is a support group for women who are addicted to married men and affairs. Groups like AA, only this one is for adulterers. Da'nessa was starting to really feel sorry for herself.

About a week later, she did receive a call from a gentleman who said he was Mr. Joseph's lawyer. She hung up the phone, but he kept calling back. He asked her to please meet with him. Fearing the worst, that maybe Michael had done something stupid like committing suicide, she agreed. When she met with the lawyer, he handed her a letter and allowed her time to read it. It was from Michael. It read as follows:

My Dearest Da'nessa,

I love you in a way I cannot explain. I never meant to hurt you. I know that I have broken your heart. Please read this letter and hopefully it will clear some things up for you. I never thought we would go beyond friendship, but that night in December, things changed. I wanted to confess to you, but it was complicated. I should have told you that I am a pastor of one of the largest churches in Middletown, Connecticut. I am not married, but I was engaged. My ex-fiancé is a kind and sweet person. Her father is a well know minister in the state of Connecticut.

I had no plans for returning to Hartford that snowy night, but I knew you were there. I wanted to tell you about the engagement and everything else I was hiding. The entire time I was in the shower, I pondered ways to tell you.

Then when I saw you standing there in front of the patio doors, I knew I had to have you. When we made love, I knew in my spirit that you gave everything. Your body, your soul, and your spirit. You made love to me like I was the most important person in the world. So I planned the trip to Las Vegas to confess everything. The first two nights, I was so caught up into being with you. I prayed for the strength to tell you. I even asked God to intervene. I needed help because my feelings were getting stronger and stronger.

Well, God intervened. Vegas was the last place I would expect to see anyone who knew me, let alone two women from my neighborhood in Middletown. When I returned, I told my ex-fiancé everything. We broke off the engagement. Then she asked that we go to counseling. I am embarrassed because I not only hurt her, but I hurt you as well. I confessed my selfishness to her.

I think about you every day. One day, I will pay for what I have done. I don't ask for forgiveness because I don't deserve it. I simply want you to understand I didn't mean to hurt anyone. I was confused and extremely selfish. I wanted the best of both worlds. The wedding is off for now. I plan to stay in counseling until I understand why I did what I did. I have never behaved so badly. From the bottom of my heart to the top of it, I am so sorry.

This letter is yours. You can take it to the media if you wish. Nothing can hurt me as much as I hurt you. I deserve whatever happens because I did you so wrong. My lawyers advised against me writing this letter and wanted to buy you off to keep this relationship a secret. I am not worth protecting. I shall never forget you as long as I live. May God's peace keep you always.

Michael Joseph

Da'nessa sat crying with the letter in her hand. She knew his words were sincere. She knew in her heart that she cared deeply for him. She had not told him about her past. So maybe God was intervening and saving him from her as well. The Lord works in mysterious ways. She knew that she would never tell a soul, for she cared for him also. Da'nessa ripped the letter into a thousand pieces. The lawyer looked at her and knew that she was in pain. She told the lawyer not to worry, she would never tell another person. She said she cared about Michael, and she wanted him happy. She stuffed the pieces of paper in the leftover coffee she was drinking and placed it in the trash container. The lawyer told Da'nessa that he had a check for ten thousand dollars. He had wanted to offer it as a way to keep her silent if word ever got out about them. He decided he could trust her, and he did not ask her to sign papers stating she will never discuss the details of their relationship. Da'nessa walked out and left the check on the table.

Da'nessa decided to do some research. She drove by the condo, but it was up for sale. She went on the Internet and discovered that not only was Michael an accomplished social worker, but he was the pastor to one of the largest Baptist congregation church in Middletown, Connecticut. He was truly engaged to the daughter of a pastor from another well-known church in the state. She is very beautiful and no doubt will make a great first lady.

Michael and Da'nessa's relationship was covered-up, and no one ever said a word. A week later, Da'nessa received the ten-thousand-dollar check in the mail. A note attached from the lawyer said enjoy it as a gift or donate it to your favorite charity. Although she was hurt and disappointed once again, Da'nessa decided she would just move on with her life. Secretly, she vowed to never let another man hurt her, no matter what. The relationship with Michael taught Da'nessa a valuable lesson. Powerful men of God just seem to be attracted to her even if she attend church or not. Da'nessa felt as though she was some type of spiritual magnet.

Da'nessa was once told, "You are a breath of fresh air. You have a regal glow about you. That brightness pulls people toward you. I don't think you realize just how captivating you are. Your warm spirit makes anyone want to be near you. You have an essence of peace." How can something so beautiful bring so much pain? Did she really have a power that was so surreal? It was hard for her to believe, but something about her always attracted strong powerful men. Da'nessa called it a soul tie or some type of spiritual attachment. Whatever it was, it was powerful. She wondered if she should fear this rare gift or learn to control it to her advantage.

She could not escape it. Maybe it was time she embrace it, ride it out just to see how far it will take her. The thought of it was confusing, but she was willing to put it to the test. Da'nessa knew this was a crazy thought. She sensed it was straight from the pits of hell. She was not a bad person. She just had some bad situation of sorts.

JOURNAL 12

Real Love Found Me

It is God who arms me with strength,
and makes my way perfect.

—Psalm 18:32 (NKJV)

It was a cool fall Connecticut morning about a year later. Da'nessa went for her normal morning walk. Nothing unusual; just the same morning walk. She would always see the same people on the walking trail. There was Mrs. Ross, an elderly widow who always took Fefe, her poodle, for a morning stroll. Mrs. Ross will often be accompanied by Mr. Rivers, whose spouse also passed away. There were many others that Da'nessa knew by face but not their names.

Everyone was friendly and seemed to look out for one another. On this particular morning, Mrs. Ross stopped Da'nessa and asked if she would be attending the neighborhood watch meeting on that Thursday. She would always remind her of the monthly meeting. "Sure, I will be there, Mrs. Ross," replied Da'nessa. "See you at seven on Thursday" were her closing remarks as Da'nessa walked away. Mrs. Ross enjoyed hosting the neighborhood watch meetings at her home. It gave her an opportunity to entertain. Something she had once enjoyed when her husband was alive.

Da'nessa arrived promptly at 7:00 p.m. on Thursday. She knew that Mrs. Ross will start the meeting on time. The meeting was crowded, which was no surprise because she served delicious meals with each meeting. The meals alone were worth the gathering. Tonight it was Italian style: lasagna made with five types of cheese, garlic bread sticks, and a garden salad. She also had several types of wine, juice, and bottle water. She never asked for any money or assistance, but everyone always left a donation in the empty cookie jar. Most stayed and helped to clean up once the meeting was adjourned.

The opening for tonight's meeting was the same. They dealt with old business first. The association was made up of about four blocks of homes and families from Gardner Avenue to Montauk Avenue, then up to Ocean Avenue. As Mr. Rivers was discussing the old business, that's when Da'nessa noticed a handsome stranger among them. A tall good-looking black police office. How could she have missed him when she first arrived? There were not that many black people at this meeting. Who was he? was her initial thought. Is he new to the neighborhood? He seemed to be looking in her direction, so she smiled and held her head down looking at her plate of food and trying to avoid direct eye contact with him. When Mr. Rivers completed the old business, Mrs. Ross came forward and introduced Officer Jerome Leary.

Officer Leary said hello to everyone and then began to share some not-so pleasant information. He reported that crime was on the upswing and that their task unit was tracking some gang-related activity in the city. He said he was speaking at different neighborhood associations asking for everyone's help. He explained the importance of reporting anything suspicious. As he spoke, Da'nessa was impressed. Not only was he good-looking, but he also spoke with intelligence. She had never seen him patrolling around in a squad car. *Where the heck did he come from?* she thought. Da'nessa had to tell herself to stay focused. With her luck, he is a pastor and married. She giggled at that thought. Then she decided to come back to earth, focus, and listen to his speech.

Officer Leary could not remain until the meeting was adjourned. He thanked everyone for their time and attention, and he left. He did leave some of his task force business card with the direct number where they could contact his unit. It was not a personal line, but it was a contact number.

After the meeting was adjourned, everyone cleaned up as usual and said their goodbyes. Da'nessa thought about Officer Leary warning and made a mental note to be more alert especially when she is out walking alone. She also pondered the thought of calling him but decided against it.

JOURNAL 13

Love

Love is patient, love is kind. It does not envy,
it does not boast, it is not proud.

—1 Corinthians 13:4 (NIV)

The Norwich Academy School system was hosting their annual fall festival on Saturday, October 30. It was a large event, and all the surrounding school's students attended. Da'nessa knew that most of her students would be there. She always enjoyed the activities. Fall was her favorite time of year. She really enjoyed the cool breeze in the air.

Da'nessa was standing at a jewelry booth trying to decide which pair of homemade earrings to purchase. They both looked great on her, but she was on a budget and only wanted one pair. As she was looking in the mirror trying to decided which one to buy, a strong deep voice said, "I like the one on the right, then again I like the one on the left also." To her surprise, when she turned to see who was talking to her, there he was Officer Leary; only he was not in his uniform. Da'nessa looked around to make sure he was talking to her and not someone else. He saw what she did: and laugh. "I was talking to you," he said to her. She had a puzzled look on her face. Then he introduced himself. "I'm sorry, my name is Jerome Leary. I remember you from the homeowner's association meeting on Gardner Avenue area. That was over a month ago, Da'nessa thought to herself. "Hi, my name is Da'nessa Baker, and it nice to meet you," she said. They both stood there awkwardly for a few minutes not knowing what to say next.

Then Da'nessa spoke. "My budget will only allow me to purchase one pair, so I must decide." She made her choice and paid the vendor.

"May I walk with you for a few minutes, if there is no one else waiting for you?" Jerome said to her. Da'nessa just smiled and said sure. As they walked and talked, Jerome explained the he had taken a job transfer from Middletown, Connecticut, to New London. He had only been there about six months when he attended their association meeting. He also told her he had hoped to meet her that night, but she would not give him direct eye contact. So he assumed she was with someone. He said he just assumed one of those gentleman might have been her husband. So he kept everything on a professional level. Then he noticed her at the festival, and she appeared to be alone. So he made his approach. Jerome was very open. Da'nessa told him that she was single, and he told her the same.

She asked what brought him out there to the school festival. He said he was actually working undercover. There had been a tip of some gang initiation, and he was there as a first line of defense. Da'nessa looked at him as if she suspected he was joking. Then he started to laugh and told her the truth. He was there with his niece who was a volunteer. He pointed in her direction and a beautiful Indian looking young lady waved back toward them. She was his niece on his ex-wife's side of the family, but he had known her since she was a baby. Before they departed from one another, they exchanged phone numbers.

Da'nessa had not expected a call from Jerome so soon, but he called the next day, which was Sunday at 3:30 p.m. They talked for three hours. He told her that he was divorced and had a son. She told him that she had never married. He thought it was kind of strange because she is a beautiful woman who is clearly in her late twenties. He didn't ask why. She volunteered some information but was mostly guarded. She shared that she had trust issues when it came to relationships.

Jerome thought that Da'nessa was a bit reserved, but something else about her puzzled him. She seemed to have a wall up, as if she were trying to protect herself from something. He loved a challenge and decided that he was going to pursue her to win over her heart. He didn't understand why he felt that way; he just knew that he had a mission.

Da'nessa liked Jerome too and decided she would take her time and see what develops. She didn't want to be his man toy. That was a role she had played too many times. Da'nessa wanted a real committed relationship. She would make him wait just to see if he was really interested. Jerome was the perfect gentleman. He treated her with kindness and respect.

Jerome was hosting a party at his home in December, and he invited Da'nessa to attend. When she arrived, the place was crowded. Jerome had a lot of friends, especially female friends. He introduced her to everyone, including his son Tyrone. His son was eight years old. Jerome had told her about his son. He had joint custody of him after his divorce. Tyrone was a very polite and well-mannered child. The party was great, but there was one guess there that seemed to unsettle Da'nessa's spirit. She is a married woman. She had four boys of her own, but neither her husband nor her sons were at the party. Her name was Wendy Kramer. She was a coworker of Jerome. They appeared to be close friends. Something about her bothered Da'nessa. Maybe it was jealousy. She is a beautiful woman.

The guest had started to leave the party. It was about 10:00 p.m. Da'nessa decided to say goodnight. She looked for Jerome and found him in the kitchen washing dishes. To her surprise, Wendy was there also. She tried not to think anything negative; after all, they are coworkers and were friends long before Jerome met her. Da'nessa told Jerome she was about to leave. Wendy said goodnight with all the fakeness she could muster up in her smile. Jerome put down his dish cloth and walked her to her car.

On her way out the door, Tyrone gave Da'nessa a big hug and said goodnight. Jerome was somewhat surprised because Tyrone doesn't take well to strangers. Yet, he seemed to like her. Jerome made a mental note of that. Da'nessa was not surprised. She had a way with children, plus she had spent most of the evening playing fun games with Tyrone while all the other adults mingled and talked among themselves. There were only three other kids at the party. Two of them were girls, and the other one was a teenage boy who appeared to be about fifteen or sixteen years old.

Jerome asked Da'nessa to call when she got home to let him know that she made it safely. They said their goodbyes, and she drove off wondering how much longer Wendy was planning on staying. It took Da'nessa about twenty minutes to make it home and unwind a few minutes before she called Jerome. When she did call, to her surprise, Wendy answered the phone. It took Da'nessa a minute to say anything. She was really taken aback by the fact that this woman felt comfortable enough to answer his phone. She told Da'nessa that Jerome was upstairs getting Tyrone ready for bed and that she would give him the message that she had called. This did not sit well with Da'nessa. Why was this married woman still at this single man's house? Where was her husband and children? Why was she feeling jealous? Da'nessa's head was swimming in confusion. She finally drifted off to sleep. Jerome never returned her call.

It was two days later, when he finally called her, she almost didn't answer the phone. She had looked at the caller ID and knew it was Jerome's number. She answered the phone with a coldest voice. Jerome was so happy-go-lucky that he sensed her tone. He asked if she was okay. Had anything happen to her? Da'nessa felt stupid for behaving in such an unlady-like manner. She apologized and told him that she had had a rough morning. Which was not true. She just didn't want to admit her jealousy.

Jerome asked if she would like to attend a movie with him later that day. He picked her up at her place around 6:00 p.m. The movie started at 6:45 p.m. The drive to the movie was quite. Jerome was sensing something was bothering Da'nessa, so he broke the silence. "Da'nessa, are you okay?" he asked. She responded with a "sure, I'm okay." Jerome did not believe her but decided not to press the issue. They both seemed to enjoy the movie. They laughed at the same moments in the movie. When the movie was over, Jerome asked if he could take her for a quick bite of food.

They went to Martello's, a Greek cafe. It's a nice little private cafe that sells the most delicious gyro sandwich, which is one of Jerome's favorite. He also knew that they had a wonderful selection of healthy foods. He knew Da'nessa loved to eat healthy. While they waited for their food to be delivered, Jerome brought up the subject again. "Something is clearly bothering you. Have I done something to upset you?" he asked Da'nessa.

She decided to be up-front with him. Da'nessa told Jerome that she felt uncomfortable with Wendy at his party. She was confused because he never returned her phone call the night of the party. Da'nessa was unsure of Jerome now. Was he playing a game with her emotions? She did not want to be caught in the middle of an affair. She had been down that road before but on the other side of the coin. She decided to put on her bold cap and asked Jerome what type of relationship he and Wendy had. Jerome smiled and asked was she jealous of another woman in his life. He saw it as flattery. She laughed with him but was serious. Jerome told Da'nessa that Wendy is just a good friend, and she had nothing to worry about. He explained that she had always been a support to him. He also emphasized to her that there had never been any intimacy between them. They were just good friends.

Jerome explained that Wendy sometimes helps to babysit Tyrone when he has to pull an all-night shift. Da'nessa asked why her husband was not at the party. Apparently, her husband Anthony had returned to his hometown in Maryland on that weekend with the kids at his grandmother's request. Da'nessa asked why Wendy didn't go with them. Jerome told her that the grandmother did not like Wendy and if she didn't have to go, she didn't.

Da'nessa had to accept his explanation. She made a mental note to keep an eye on this Wendy woman. Da'nessa and Jerome's relationship changed after that conversation. He was very mindful not to mention Wendy around her and declined most invites that he knew Wendy would be attending. Da'nessa was very pleased with their relationships and allowed things to advance. Da'nessa even offered to keep Tyrone if Jerome had overnight duty. She and Tyrone really took to one another. He was glad to be with her when his dad had to work. Jerome had hoped to get full custody of his son. The judge leaned toward the mother having custody because she had remarried and provided a more stable home. Life with his mother was good, but Tyrone loved being with his dad. He was proud that his dad was a police officer. All the kids thought it was cool when his dad stopped by their neighborhood or visit his school.

The holidays were approaching. Da'nessa decided to go home to her family for Christmas. Jerome asked her to attend a Thanksgiving dinner with him at his job. It was a tradition among the police officers. They believed no one should be alone on Thanksgiving, including those on duty. There was one rule: no alcohol. As expected, Wendy and her husband Anthony was at the dinner. Their boys were not with them. Jerome introduced Da'nessa to everyone. They were all friendly and kind.

Da'nessa went to the restroom. She was in a restroom stall when she overheard two women talking. They were not aware that she had entered. One lady said to the other, "I bet Wendy is upset tonight." "Yes," said the other one. They continued to gossip, saying, "Everyone knows that Jerome and she are secret lovers. That's why she transferred here after he got the job promotion and relocated. Who the heck do they think they are kidding?"

"Well, I'm glad he has a new woman," said one of the ladies. "He is a good guy."

"True," said the other one, "everyone in the Middletown precinct is still talking about the nerve of that woman. She drives back and forth every day. Her husband must have someone on the side because he doesn't seem to care." It was a scene directly out of a soap opera, Da'nessa thought.

"They say he is a saint," said the other lady. "He is so religious and so forgiving. He loves those boys and will do anything for them. How funny." The other woman said, "The devil and the saint." They both laughed and walked out of the restroom.

Da'nessa sat there for a few minutes trying to absorb what she just overheard. Maybe they knew she was there and wanted her to know. Her head was spinning. She could not allow Jerome to see her like this, especially after the last time they had gathered for his house party. He might think she is paranoid. Da'nessa pulled herself together, put on a fake smile, and walked out of the restroom. Jerome was talking to Anthony and Wendy when she approached them. He asked if she was okay. She told him that she had shared some small talk with a nice lady in the restroom. He smiled and took hold of her hand. Wendy's eyes glanced down at their hands. Da'nessa decided to spice things up a little, so she moved closer to Jerome, and he gave her a warm, affectionate hug.

Da'nessa felt that it was time to make this a real relationship. She had not made love to Jerome, and they had been dating almost a year. It had been ten months and two days. Something he always joked about. Jerome had never pressured her to make love, which often made her wonder if he was being cared for somewhere else. Then she told herself that maybe he is truly a gentleman. Jerome had told her over and over that he wanted her for more than just her body. As they were leaving the dinner, Jerome jokingly asked Da'nessa if she wanted to go to his house for a nightcap. Da'nessa said yes, which was a shock and a surprise to him. He had asked her over once or twice after a date in the past, but she always declined. She only seems comfortable being over there when it was Tyrone's weekend to visit. This was her safety net.

Jerome kept a superclean house which surprised her for a man. He had been raised by his mother who was a widow. She worked and attended college part-time. So he took on the responsible for the upkeep of the home. He was also a very good cook. Jerome was a complete package. He was tall, handsome, clean, and a great cook; plus he had a good job.

She liked him, and she knew it. Why was she dragging her feet with this one? Had he been a married pastor, would she have slept with him by now? She wondered in the back of her mind. Truthfully, the answer is no. He is special and different. Thank God, he is not a married man. *Anyway, tonight would be the night,* she thought. If he made his move toward lovemaking, she will accept his advances. She was mentally and physically ready to make love to Jerome.

"What is your desired drink?" he asked her after putting their coats away. The house was warm and cozy, but he turned on the gas fireplace and some nice slow Luther Vandross music on the speaker system. The music was piped throughout the house. He knew that she was crazy about Luther's music. She had a glass of Riesling wine. He knew she like white wine, so he kept some in the house. He decided to have a Lowenbrau beer. They sat and made small talk for about an hour.

As the drinks slowly mellowed her, she laughed, talked, and relaxed. He looked deep into her eyes and asked if he could kiss her. It was a strange question because he had kissed her many times before, but something was different this time. "Yes, you may kiss me," she said. Jerome kissed her passionately. Then he rubbed his hand on her right cheek and kissed her again. His kiss had intense feelings attached. She was so relaxed by his touch that she had not noticed his hands caressing her all over. His touch felt good, and she did not want him to stop. They had been sitting on this warm plush shag carpet in front of the fireplace. He leaned her back on the soft rug and continued to caress her. He looked deep into her soul as he touched her. She felt his desire for her. Then for a brief second, she thought about Rupert. To her surprise, the next words that came from his lips were "may I make love to you." She responded with a yes. Jerome slowly unzipped her dress and eased it down her shoulders. Da'nessa had on beautiful lace undergarment. She loved beautiful underclothing. Jerome kissed her shoulders. His touch excited her. Jerome nibbled on her eye lobe as he slid the remainder of her dress off. "You have a lovely body," he told her as he examined her. "Your skin is so soft, it's unreal."

As Da'nessa lay there on the floor in her lovely garments, she watched Jerome undress. He removed his shirt and silk T-shirt. He had a hairy chest that was strong and well-defined. She was totally mesmerized by this man. Jerome lay beside her on the floor. She was lying on her back by now, and he smiled at her as he admired how lovely she was. He wanted to take his time and remember this moment forever. He began to kiss her again.

"I have often dreamed of this moment," he said. "Now that it's happening, I want to enjoy every second." Da'nessa was speechless and emotional. As the foreplay continued, her heart was pounding with excitement. He asked, "How can I please you?"

She said, "Just being here with you is pleasure enough." Then they made love there in front of the fireplace. Jerome was very concerned and purposed in his heart to be gentle. Jerome got to his feet, and then he picked Da'nessa up and took her to the bedroom. He placed her in bed and put the covers over her. His bed was supersoft; it was a California king-size with a big down comforter. There was even a fireplace in his bedroom. He really had good taste. Jerome returned from shutting off the lights in the house. He climbed into bed with Da'nessa and held her until they both fell asleep.

The next morning, they woke up to snow. Da'nessa had the day off, and Jerome didn't have work until 6:00 p.m. They lay in bed watching the snow that had started late last night. It was 8:00 a.m. Da'nessa went to the restroom. She had not planned on staying the night, but here she was an overnight guest. Jerome told her that he had extra toothbrushes in the bathroom closet. She took a green one, which is her favorite color and brushed her teeth. Then she washed her face. Da'nessa decided to take a shower. She asked if it was okay. When she came out the shower, Jerome had made her a cup of coffee and a bowl of cut fruit on a tray. Both were her favorites. He gave her one of his T-shirts to put on. She sat at the small sitting area in his bedroom near the fireplace that he had lit. Everything was magical. How could she not like such a wonder guy? Maybe even fall in love with him one day.

Jerome was in the shower when he heard the show door open. Da'nessa had gotten back in the shower with him. It was a large beautiful shower with a waterfall showerhead and mood lights that vibrated to the sound of music. It had surround sound in the shower. As Da'nessa caressed his back with soap, Jerome was shocked, but he was truly enjoying it. They spent almost an hour in the shower just exploring one another. They got out of the shower, and he took a giant-size towel and dried her off. They made love again, but this time something strange happened. "What in the world just happened?" he said in a small voice that Da'nessa overheard.

"I don't know," she said, "but I felt it too." "It felt like our spirits were released" Jerome said. She knew exactly what he felt because she felt it too. Never had she made love so deeply that she released her spirit, and never had he felt so connected to someone while making love. The two of them lay in bed and drifted off to sleep. When they awoke again, it was noon. Da'nessa asked Jerome to take her home. He showered and got dressed in his uniform. He decided to go in early to relieve some of the overnight staff. This is not unusual. The police force is like a brotherhood, and with the snow falling, he knew they could use the extra hands.

When they got to Da'nessa's house, he walked Da'nessa to her door. Then he decided to shovel snow from her walkway and put sand and salt on it. She went in and changed into comfortable clothing and made him some hot chocolate and sandwiches. They ate the sandwiches and drank the hot beverage. She also made a healthy lunch for him to take to work. He asked her if he could see her on Sunday, his off day. He wanted her to go to church with him in Middletown, if the weather permitted. He also wanted her to meet his mother. She agreed but was really nervous. They kissed one another for a long minute and said their goodbye. He promised to call her on his break.

Jerome reported to work around 4:00 p.m. He was early, but the guys were glad to see him. One of the overnight guys had left early because his wife went into labor. She was four weeks early, and everyone was concerned for the baby. He had gone directly to the hospital because her parents had driven her there. They shared a duplex home with her parents, which was great. Jerome was glad he came in early also. He had a lot on his mind. He was still puzzled about what had happened between him and Da'nessa as they made love that morning. Everyone in the office commented on how beautiful they thought Da'nessa was. Some even said she had a beautiful spirit. Everyone seemed happy for him, but Wendy. Her mood was lukewarm toward Jerome. He noticed the difference and decided to avoid her. He knew that their friendship bothered Da'nessa, so he decided that maybe it was time he and Wendy put some space between them.

A call came in requesting police assistance at a senior home in the area. Jerome signed out a squad car and answered the call. Apparently, some squatters were sleeping in the basement doorway at the senior home. They had been asked to leave prior, but the staff discovered they had returned an hour later. So they called the police.

Jerome knew they were cold and needed a place to stay. He took them in his squid car to the local shelter on the other side of town. Because it had been snowing, the shelter allowed them to check in from the cold. Jerome was riding around patrolling the area when his personal pager rang. He didn't like to answer his pager while on duty. It was Wendy's desk number on the caller ID. He decided not to respond. She called three more times within the hour.

Jerome had been patrolling for about three hours when he decided it was time for a quick break. He radioed his break intentions to the dispatcher and stopped at the local coffee shop. He knew they had clean restrooms, and he was also fond of the staff. After using the restroom, he returned Wendy's call. By now, she was headed out the office to go home in Middletown. She answered her desk phone. She asked Jerome was he mad at her. He knew it was a game she was playing. "No" was his reply. "Why would I be mad at you? Have you done something I am not aware of?" Jerome asked.

"No," she said, "it's just that you barely spoke to me earlier. I guess you had a long night, huh!" was her next remark.

He knew she was being sarcastic. So he changed the subject. "Where are you?" he asked. "I'm headed home. I came in early to work a few hours." She changed the subject by remarking, "Everyone has been talking about your wonderful lady friend." She said this in a cold tone. They all seemed to like her, especially the guys. Jerome smiled to himself. "Yah, she is pretty terrific." Wendy did not like that comment.

"I guess you don't need my friendship now that you have miss terrific," she said.

"Are you jealous, Mrs. Anthony Kramer?" Jerome said.

"No!" she said quickly. "Any way I've got to get on the road home before things get pretty bad up that way, I will talk to you later," she said as she ended the call. "Okay, goodbye."

What a piece of jealous work she is, Jerome thought to himself. Coworkers had complained about her before, but this was the first time he really noticed her behaviors.

JOURNAL 14

Blending Families

He who finds a wife finds a good thing, And
obtains favor from the Lord.

—Proverbs 18:22 (NKJV)

Sunday arrived way too soon. The weather was beautiful. It had not snowed since Friday. The one time Da'nessa was begging for snow, none came. Jerome picked her up at 9:00 a.m. They would drive to his mother's place, then the three of them will leave for church. Da'nessa changed clothing about four times. Nothing seemed right. She looked great in whatever she wore. She had gotten her hair done Saturday. Getting her hair done always made her feel confident about herself. Meeting his mother stripped her of all confidence. Why was she nervous? She and Jerome were just friends.

His mother's home is beautiful, she thought as they drove up the driveway. No wonder he had such great taste. He opened the car door for Da'nessa to get out. Jerome was always the perfect gentleman. He had a key to his mom's place, and he opened the front door and announced that he was home. His mother yelled down to him from upstairs, "Down in a minute, sweetheart." She sounded very proper. Danessa laughed to herself. That what people say about her, as well when they talk to her on the phone. In her hometown, they always said she spoke proper.

When Vernita Leary came down the stairs, you would have thought she just stepped out of a fashion magazine. She looked like a combination of the actress Diahann Carroll and Lynn Whitfield. She is beautiful and lovely for a woman in her sixties.

Jerome smiled really big as he embraced his mother and said good morning. He then turned and introduced his mother. "Mom, this is Da'nessa Baker," he said. His mother extended her hand to say hello to Da'nessa. Vernita looked at Da'nessa with a slight look of surprise. Then she turned to Jerome and said, "Yes, I can see it clearly."

Da'nessa was puzzled by the remark and look at Jerome. He smiled and said, "Wait one second, and I will explain." He went into the other room and returned with an old photo book. He opened the book and showed Da'nessa some pictures. The woman on the picture looked just like Da'nessa, but that was impossible. She had never taken a photo in a wedding dress with a guy she didn't know. Da'nessa was confused.

Jerome explained. "This is my mother and father on their wedding day." Da'nessa looked exactly like Vernita when she was young. Jerome had told his mother about the resemblance when he had visited a few months earlier. He had not told Da'nessa because he didn't want to frighten her. Things felt weird for Vernita and Da'nessa, mainly because both women admired the same man standing before them.

They departed for church. Da'nessa offered to get in the back seat, but Vernita insisted she ride in the front, although they were driving her Mercedes SUV. Church was crowded. When it was time for visitors to stand, Da'nessa stood with five other visitors. The pastor of the church seemed to stare in her direction. She looked down at Jerome to avoid the pastor's stare. After service, Jerome insisted he had to introduce her to the pastor. Da'nessa was fearful of her strong attraction to pastor's. As it turned out, the pastor was Jerome's uncle. His mother's bother. He had a strong presence in Jerome's life. The visit turned out to be a really good visit.

Vernita was very kind to Da'nessa, and they seem to really get along well. The ride home was good, and they talked and laughed the entire way. When they got to her place, Da'nessa asked him if he would like to stay the night. Jerome was happy and certainly wanted to be there with her. They made love and fell asleep. The alarm went off at 5:00 a.m. Da'nessa got up and took a shower. She had to get dressed for work. Jerome was still asleep.

He woke as she was about to leave. She told him to stay in bed, and she gave him a spare key to lock up. She gave him a long kiss before she left. She had written him a note. She had remembered how sweet it was when Michael had left her a note the first night she had stayed with him.

Da'nessa often wondered about Michael and prayed that he was well. Jerome woke up about 11:00 a.m. He saw the note addressed to him and the key to lock up. He thought her note was very sweet and made a mental note to send her some flowers at work. Da'nessa had decided to go home to Georgia for Christmas. She had not seen her Grandma Bessie in a long time. She needed time with her family. She needed to talk to Ma Bessie about some spiritual things that have been happening since she met Jerome. Ma Bessie was very spiritual, and Da'nessa trusted her wisdom.

Jerome and Da'nessa decided to celebrate their Christmas when she returned from Georgia a week later. She did leave some Christmas gifts for Tyrone at his place. He and Tyrone will be spending some time on Christmas Day at his mother's home in Middletown. Jerome took her to the airport to catch her flight. Normally, she would be so excited and ready to go home, but this time she had mixed emotions. She really ached inside, knowing that she would be away from Jerome. He too would miss her. He feared he would never see her again. How could he feel this way? She was only flying to Georgia to visit family for a week.

The flight home was not good. The weather had taken a turn for the worse over the Washington, DC area. They had lots of turbulences. It was a rocky and scary flight. Da'nessa was glad when the plane touched down in Atlanta. She still had one more flight to catch. This would be on a smaller plane to Valdosta, Georgia. At least, the weather had cleared up some.

Da'nessa's father met her at the airport in Valdosta. He had a really sad look on his face. She knew something was not right. Her dad always greets everyone with a smile. "Dad, what's wrong?" Da'nessa asked. "I can see it on your face," she remarked.

"It's Ma Bessie, they had to rush her to the hospital this morning. It does not look good. Everyone thinks she is holding on to see you." Da'nessa begin to cry and felt a pain so deep in her soul. This pain was one she had never experienced before. Her dad took her directly to the hospital. She tried to put on a brave face. When she saw her Ma Bessie lying there with all those tubes coming out of her small body, Da'nessa cried uncontrollably. Da'nessa's mom and other relatives were there in the waiting room. She gave her mother a big hug.

Ma Bessie must have sensed Da'nessa in the area or she heard the commotions because she opened her eyes. She smiled at Danessa and whispered, "I have been waiting for you." Danessa moved in closer and gave her a kiss on the forehead. She playfully told her great grandmother, "I'm here so you can get out of this hospital bed because I have a lot to talk about with you." Da'nessa loved talking to Ma Bessie. Even when she was a little girl, she would spend her days on the porch talking to Ma Bessie and brushing her long pretty hair.

Da'nessa noticed that Ma Bessie's eyes were the color of a blue marble. Ma Bessie's eyes were always light brown, but now they were blue. Glassy blue! Something has changed them. "Why are your eyes blue?" she asked. Ma Bessie explained the death angel had come. "They came for me the other day, and I told them no." she said. "I had to see my Da'nessa before I depart. I refused to go because I knew I would see you one last time," she told her granddaughter.

"Who came to get you, Ma Bessie?" she asked.

"The death angels, and they show me the path to the light tunnel. It's a beautiful section of space. It was among the stars, and it was serene. The sky made a sweet melody. It glowed the most beautiful shades of the rainbow. I was tempted to go at that moment," said Ma Bessie with a glossy look on her face. "But I needed so much to say goodbye to you." The death angel granted her request and allowed her to wait for Da'nessa visit. "Somehow they knew I need to let you know that I was going to be okay. I know how much you worry about me," Ma Bessie said.

They both smiled. Da'nessa did not want Ma Bessie to leave her and go into the heavens. But she knew she was being selfish. Ma Bessie had lived on earth close to one hundred years. They loved one another so much. Da'nessa knew Ma Bessie's body was tired. Da'nessa stayed at the hospital with Ma Bessie all night. She did not want to leave her side. Ma Bessie did feel better, but she and her doctors knew that it was just a matter of time. There was nothing else they could do. Since it was close to Christmas, the family asked if she could be released to home care.

Ma Bessie wanted to be at home when the angels returned to get her. She was released under hospice care. There really was no need for nurse's care because her family loved her so much, and they attended to her every need, especially Da'nessa. She even crawled in bed with Ma Bessie from time to time to talk or just sleep beside her.

During one of those moments, she told her about Jerome. Ma Bessie seems to already know. She said she saw the love glow on Da'nessa when she was at the hospital. "What is the love glow?" asked Da'nessa. Ma Bessie explained, "When two people meet and they are soul mates, once they consummate their love, their spirits bond, and they light a love glow." She then asked Da'nessa a very personal question, "When you made love to Jerome, did you experience something that felt like your spirit had left you, and did he experience the same thing?"

Da'nessa was shocked. "Yes, Ma Bessie, it happened, and I had planned to ask you about it." Ma Bessie asked to see her right hand. Da'nessa knew what she was about to do. Ma Bessie is part of the native American Indians. Ma Bessie is also a Christian, but she still believed in the old spiritual ways of her people. Ma Bessie was about to peek into her future. "Da'nessa, he will make you very happy for many years," she said, "but there will be two major tests. One you will survive, but the other will tear your heart out. Do not lose all hope, for you will be happy again." Then Ma Bessie closed Da'nessa's hand and said, "We will speak no more about this. That is all I can tell you. I will share this with you. You will see me again after my death, and that will be the day you give birth to your baby girl." Da'nessa eyes lit up. She knew Ma Bessie's words were true. She never did a reading until it was time, no matter how hard the other person begged.

It was now two days till Christmas, and Da'nessa still had no clue what to get Jerome. He had everything. She knew he loved basketball, and he especially enjoyed the Atlanta Hawks. She decided to purchase him some of their official gear and take back to Connecticut. She and Jerome talked daily, and he really missed her. She had to admit she really missed him also. He always asked about Ma Bessie's health. He knew how close they were. Things with Ma Bessie seem to improve. Da'nessa's time at home was great, but it came time when she had to return to Connecticut. Da'nessa was torn. She wondered in her heart of hearts if she would ever see Ma Bessie alive again. She wanted to stay until the end, but no one knew when the end would come. Da'nessa had to be realistic. She had a life in Connecticut, and she needed to return there. Ma Bessie insisted she return to Connecticut.

Jerome met her at the airport. Her flight had been delayed in Atlanta, so she did not arrive until after midnight. He didn't care he would have waited all night if he had to just see her and hold her in his arms. As she exited the terminal, he saw her and his heart skipped a beat. He had never been so happy to see someone. She felt the same, and it seemed as though they had been apart for ages, but it had only been a week. He picked her up and gave her the biggest kiss. She can tell she was missed. They decided to go back to his place. He had checked on her place all week. He had watered her plants and even dusted her furniture. *He really is an amazing guy*, she thought.

Jerome was glad to hold her in his arms. She had had a long flight. She wanted to shower and get in bed. He offered to make her a hot bubble bath, but she wanted a shower instead. He could tell that she was tired. Da'nessa got into the shower, and as the water ran down her back, she felt his strong hands apply soap. His touch felt so good. She missed his touch and decided to press her body next to his.

He held her from behind as the water cascaded over them. Jerome began to kiss her. They made love although she was tired.

Then he whispered something she had not expected. He said, "I love you." He had never said those three words to her. She pulled away and faced him. She looked deep into his eyes and said I love you too. He was so emotional at that moment that tears formed in his eyes. He knew then and there that he really wanted to spend the rest of his life with this woman.

The next morning, Da'nessa awoke to the smell of breakfast. She loved the smell of coffee because it reminded her of Ma Bessie's house years ago. Jerome had laid out a new beautiful gown and robe for her. She smiled, washed up, and put it on. It fit perfect. Men always knew how to fit her in lingerie. She went downstairs and gave him a big hug. "Good morning, did you rest well?" he asked.

"Very well, thanks. What about you?"

"I slept like a baby," was his response.

"I hope I didn't snore last night. I was so tired," she said. They both laughed and then enjoyed the breakfast. She also thanked him for the lovely gift. They decided to exchange their Christmas gifts. He gave her a beautiful pair of diamond earrings. She loved them. She gave him the Atlanta Hawks gear, and he was overjoyed. He was determined to wear it all on the same day.

JOURNAL 15

Wedding Plans

Therefore what God has joined together,
let no one separate.

—Mark 10:9 (NIV)

Their relationship really picked up, and by Valentine's Day they were engaged to get married. Da'nessa was so happy to call back home and tell her family, especially Ma Bessie. They decided to take a trip to South Georgia during her spring break so that Jerome could meet her family. He had met her mom and dad when they came to Connecticut for a visit at the end of January.

Jerome wanted to meet Ma Bessie. Her health would not allow her to travel. The drive to South Georgia took eighteen hours, but because they were together, it seemed like much less. They did stopover in Virginia for the night. They stayed with one of his college classmates.

When they arrived, they went directly to see Ma Bessie before going to rest. Ma Bessie commented on how handsome and tall Jerome was. All the women in the family felt that he was handsome. Jerome could see that Da'nessa was Ma Bessie's heart. The two of them smiled and giggled the entire visit. Ma Bessie also saw Jerome's love glow, and she knew that he was the one for her Da'nessa. She also knew some things she dared not share with them.

Ma Bessie told Jerome that she wanted to speak with him in private. She asked Da'nessa to leave the room. Da'nessa joked with Ma Bessie, "Please be gentle on him. He knows I'm your heart." Da'nessa went in the kitchen and joined her mom. "It's time for the famous talk," said her mom with a smile on her face.

"What does she talk about?" Da'nessa asked. "You will never know. It is for him and him alone. Do not ask because he will refuse. If he breaks his promise and share it with you, it will bring bad luck on the marriage, or so they say. Therefore, you must never ask, and he must never tell."

Her mother said, "The words they share will bless your marriage in the end." Da'nessa had never heard her mother speak this way, but she knew that what she said was the truth. Her family has lots of traditions, and they take them very seriously.

Jerome sat next to Ma Bessie, and she reached out and held his hand. He had a strange sensation when she touched him. It was as if she read his spiritual aura. "I'm going to share some things with you. It is our family way. You are not to tell Da'nessa any of this, and she will know not to ask you. I promise it will bless your marriage in the long-term." Jerome agreed to the terms.

Then Ma Bessie said, "Adultery can destroy a marriage. Even the appearance of adultery is bad, but when it's your soul mate, they will forgive you. Please remember this when times get tough. You have a good heart, and you care about my baby. You will create a bad situation out of spite. Something that you will regret and carry the shame. We all carry those types of guilt. No one is perfect. You must forgive yourself." Her words puzzled Jerome. He continued to listen.

Ma Bessie told him the following, "Protect Da'nessa's heart at all cost, and she will love you until death do part you." She placed her hand on his head and did an old Indian prayer chant. Jerome was very respectful of Ma Bessie's traditions. "I have embedded these words in your thoughts. You will forget them, but when the time is right, they will come forth." Jerome didn't know what to say or think.

He didn't know how to accept what she was telling him. None of it made any sense.

The wedding was set for May 6. It would be held in Middletown, Connecticut, at his uncle's church. Jerome's uncle would officiate the ceremony. Ma Bessie's health had taken a turn for the worst, and she was not able to attend. Two weeks earlier, she had been given the okay to fly by her doctor, but now she had fluid in her lungs and could not travel. They would video the wedding and e-mail part of it to her so that she could watch it that night.

It was a beautiful ceremony. Everything was perfect, except there were two couples on the guest list that bother Da'nessa. They were Mr. and Mrs. Anthony Kramer. She didn't mind Anthony being there, but she just didn't like or trust Wendy Kramer. The other couple was Reverend and Mrs. Michael Joseph. She was shocked to learn that Jerome and Michael were classmates and lifelong friends.

When Michael and his wife approached the couple at the reception, he said hello to Da'nessa. Jerome was surprised that they knew one another. Michael explained that they had worked together at the Capitol Building in Hartford. The couple continued to greet their guest as the line moved on into the reception. The reception hall was decorated beautifully in cream and gold. It was very regal.

They made a small video clip for Ma Bessie, and it was e-mailed to her. One of the younger family members opened the e-mail for Ma Bessie, and she got to see the parts of the wedding and reception. Ma Bessie cried the entire time. She knew that Da'nessa will be okay, and she can let go now. Ma Bessie knew in her heart that she was holding on for her. Three months later, on August 3, Ma Bessie passed away. Her death was peaceful. She died in her sleep on Da'nessa's birthday.

JOURNAL 16

Growing Family

Then God blessed them and said to them,
"Be fruitful and multiply.

—Genesis 1:28

Jerome and Da'nessa had been married for a year, and they were expecting their first child together. Da'nessa loved Tyrone and treated him like he was her own son, but the news of their pregnancy brought excitement in the house. It was the end of July, and the weather was hot and unbearable for a pregnant woman. They had decided not to inquire about the sex of the baby; whatever they were blessed with, they would be happy. Besides, they had heard so many horror stories about the wrong gender predictions. Da'nessa had managed to work out during her pregnancy. She refused to gain a lot of weight. She swam a lot because she wanted her muscles to stay toned.

A full moon was due on August 2, and it was two days away. She always joked with Jerome about her family's ways. This time, it was not a joke. Da'nessa was starting to have contractions. They timed the contractions, and they were about fifteen minutes apart. They called her doctor, and he said if they reached eight minutes apart, then come into the hospital. When the contractions reached ten minutes apart, Jerome panicked and insisted they go to the hospital.

Da'nessa was calm as the ocean breeze. After three hours at the hospital, they were sent home. Her contractions had stopped. She was only having what is known as Braxton-Hicks or false labor pains. When they returned home, it was around eight o'clock. Da'nessa told her husband that she was tired and wanted to get some sleep. He decided to stay up and watch sports. Da'nessa fell asleep quickly because she was exhausted. She began to dream that she was sitting on Ma Bessie's porch back home in Georgia. It was a cool breeze in the air, and she was very much pregnant. As Da'nessa rocked back and forth in Ma Bessie's favorite rocking chair, Ma Bessie walked out of the house and joined her. She had two glasses of peach ice tea in her hands. She knew that Da'nessa loved peach ice tea.

"Ma Bessie, what are you doing here?" she asked. "You know you died last August."

"I know," said Ma Bessie, "but I came to tell you it's time." Ma Bessie put her hands on Da'nessa's stomach. "It's time for the baby, and it's a girl." At that moment in the dream, Da'nessa's water broke. Strangely, her water really broke, and she woke up in a wet bed. She got to her feet and slowly walked to where Jerome was watching the game. "Honey, we need to go back to the hospital. My water just broke," she managed to say between the contractions.

Jerome jumped up and ran in circles trying to decide what to do first. Da'nessa caught his arm and held him still for a moment. "Call the doctor first, honey," she said. "I'm going to take a quick shower and change out these wet clothing. You get the car." She was in such control that it amazed him. He did as she said, and soon they were on their way to the hospital.

When they arrived at the emergency room, a nurse met them with a wheelchair. As soon as Da'nessa sat in the chair, a gush of water poured from her body. She was so embarrassed. She didn't know that more water could come out of your amniotic sac after your birth water has broken. The nurse told her no need to apologize; they see it all the time.

By the time Jerome parked the car and reached her, she was assigned to a maternity room and was hooked up to a monitor. The monitor showed every time she was about to have a contraction. In between contraction, she told him about the dream and what Ma Bessie had said about the baby and that it was a girl.

Da'nessa also remembered that while she was alive, Ma Bessie had told her she would return that night. How could she have known unless she really was an angel and she was watching over them? Ma Bessie will always be an angel in Da'nessa's eyes. On August 3 at half past two in the morning, Caressa De'Nay Leary was born. It was exactly one year ago that Ma Bessie had passed away.

This was a sign to Da'nessa. Caressa had Ma Bessie's soul. Jerome was happy, but he also knew that Ma Bessie had shared some words with him. He dared not discuss them with Da'nessa, and she never once asked. For now, he just wanted to enjoy life and this new addition to the family.

Caressa and Da'nessa shared the same birthday, which they both happened to have that special day with Ma Bessie. Who had crossed over to the spirit world on that same date. The three of them were truly connected in more ways than anyone could ever imagine.

By Caressa's third birthday, it was clear that she was a very bright child. She loved her daddy, and he loved her, but she especially loved her older brother Tyrone. He was superprotective of his little princess. That's what he called her: his little princess sister. He read to her and played games with her. They were one big happy family.

JOURNAL 17

Foretold Truth

Then you will know the truth,
and the truth will set your free.

—John 8:32 (NIV)

Things between Jerome and Da'nessa were not so good. He had been working longer hours lately. They seem to have lost interest in the bedroom. Maybe it was Da'nessa's fault. Jerome was very suspicious of her and Michael Joseph. He felt that they had something between them that he could not understand. They didn't see each other often, but on those rare occasions when they did, they seem uncomfortable, as if they were hiding a secret.

At first, he thought it was because of the racial difference. But they had other friends that were not African American, and they all got along well. Plus, she really had fun with his coworkers, most of whom were Caucasians. They were at the Fourth of July outing, and Michael was there without his wife. She was pregnant with their fourth child and could not bear the heat. So she stayed home.

All the men had been playing tennis while the ladies sat on the sidelines under the shade of the tents. Michael had finished his game which he lost, and Jerome was still playing. Jerome looked over and noticed that Michael had taken a seat near Da'nessa. He could clearly see that they were talking about something important. Jerome finished and came over to where Da'nessa was sitting. When he approached, Michael walked off. He asked his wife what just happened. She said nothing, he was just worried about his wife and the unborn baby. She had just lied to her husband. For some strange reason, she always felt the need to lie to Jerome about her and Michael's past relationship. He had asked her about it several times over the past few years since their wedding.

Jerome decided to approach Michael for answers. He had a strange feeling concerning his wife and his friend. The guys decided to meet for lunch. Da'nessa did not know about the meeting. Jerome did not beat around the bush. He asked him directly if he and his wife had something going on. Michael asked if he really wanted to know the truth, and Jerome said yes. Michael told him that he and Da'nessa had a love relationship years ago. He explained that it was before he was married and before Jerome had met Da'nessa. This news hit him deep in his guts. Why had she lied? If this was before they married, why keep it a secret? Honestly, this was before she knew Jerome, so why conceal it? He wondered if she still had feelings for Michael.

Michael continued with his story. He told how they were good friends who worked at the Capitol in Hartford and how he had developed feelings for her, but by this time, he had already gotten engaged. Michael said he had wanted Da'nessa as well as his wife. He said that Da'nessa didn't know he was a minister or that he was engaged. Michael admitted he was very confused in those days. He made his decision based upon what his family expected. The saddest part of the whole story was how Da'nessa found out and what had happened in Las Vegas. Michael said that he hated himself for years and wanted so much to find her and apologize in person. He said when he got the wedding invitation, he was hoping it was a different Da'nessa, but when he saw her at the wedding, he knew it was her.

He said he prayed that he had not ruined her wedding day by being there. He was too embarrassed to leave, and he could never explain to his wife why they had to leave the wedding of his dear friend. Jerome asked Michael if he still had feelings for Da'nessa.

He said yes; he wish he didn't, but he does, but not in a lustful way. He just really valued their friendship they once shared. He asked what they were talking about on the Fourth of July at the tennis match. Michael said he had asked her why she had not told Jerome about their brief relationship. Jerome had a right to know that they were once lovers. Why was she hiding it? He had told his wife the night of Jerome and Da'nessa's wedding? He felt bad for Da'nessa, and he didn't want to keep secrets from Jerome because they were old friends. He had hoped the four of them could talk about it openly. He needed peace and felt that as long as Jerome didn't know, there could be no peace in the friendship. Jerome thanked Michael for his honesty. He needed time to think. He knew he had to approach Da'nessa concerning this matter. Why had she kept it a secret? Did she still have feelings for Michael? Did her heart not belong to him? None of this made any sense to him. This bothered Jerome for a week. He did not touch his wife or make love to her. She knew something was not right but decided to leave well enough alone.

Carissa stayed the night with Nana Vernita, her grandmother. She insisted upon the title Nana instead of Grandmother. Tyrone was with his mom. Da'nessa decided to make a candlelight dinner for her and Jerome. Everything was beautiful, and she wore a lovely red dress that he had brought her. Jerome came home and showered. He was a little perturbed but decided to play along and dress for the occasion. She made his favorite food, rack of lamb with rosemary, kale and mango salad with hot butter rolls. She even had his favorite beer. As they sat down to eat, he asked her again, "Tell me what is going on between you and Michael."

"Nothing," she yelled. "Why can't you just accept that. When I asked you about Wendy, you said nothing was going on, and I accepted your answer all though I knew differently." The fight had begun; neither hid their frustration.

"What are you talking about?" he said with a mad look on his face.

"I know that you and Wendy are lovers. Everyone at your job knows." Da'nessa said this while fuming. "I didn't make a big deal over that," she shouted at him. Jerome was pissed and told her flat-out that he never slept with Wendy. Then he said, to add insult to injury, "I could have had sex with her many times, but I chose not to. I respect her husband and their marriage. Regardless of the gossip at work, you should know I'm a better person than that," Jerome yelled. Da'nessa knew her husband was telling the truth. I guess you don't really know your own husband and I don't know my wife."

She just looked at him with a wild stare as he said this. "Why are you keeping secrets about your relationship with Michael Joseph?" he said with a cold look in his eyes.

"What secrets?" said Da'nessa.

"Now you are lying to me? Michael told me everything, including what happened in Las Vegas," said Jerome.

Da'nessa had a shocked look on her face. She pulled away from the dining room table and stood up. She then looked Jerome in the face and said, "That jerk Michael has ruined my life once again." She went into the bedroom and locked the door. Her response surprised Jerome and caused him to become even more angry. Maybe she cared about Michael more than she was admitting. Da'nessa heard Jerome's car pull out of the garage. She cried with a cry that could not be comforted. She knew that her life with Jerome would never be the same again. Da'nessa questioned herself. Why was she ashamed to admit to her husband that she and Michael had something special once?

Da'nessa wanted to hate Michael. She told herself not to have anything else to do with him, but she knew all too well that this was her fault. She had too much pride. She convinced herself that she should hate Michael with a level of hate she had never felt before. Why didn't Michael just leave things alone? Who cares that he had guilt? He had chosen his perfect little wife who had their perfect little kids. The truth was Da'nessa was mad at herself for the various mistakes she had made throughout the years of her life.

Da'nessa knew in her heart that she was in the wrong. She had behaved selfishly. She knew she should have told Jerome day one about Michael, but her pride had gotten the best of her. She knew she no longer had feelings for Michael. She was just ashamed of her past, and this was the first time it had caught up with her. She now feared that that rest of her past might catch up as well.

Jerome came home later that night, and Da'nessa was still locked in their bedroom. He decided to sleep in the guest room. They did not communicate for several days, even after Caressa came home. He decided to talk with his mother about a possible separation. He was having a difficult time trusting his wife. Did she have other things she was hiding? Vernita, Jerome's mom, disagreed. She told Jerome to keep the family together for the children. She recommended that they go to marriage counseling.

Lately, Jerome hated to go home except to see Caressa. Jerome knew he loved Da'nessa and decided he wanted his family. Whatever she was hiding was her past, and he was sure they could work it out with some counseling. He stayed in the home and hoped one day they would work through this difficult time. Maybe this was the true test that Ma Bessie had told him about, but there was no evidence of adultery.

It had been two months, and they barely spoke a word to one another. Jerome decided to go to a fiftieth birthday party for one of his co-worker's without Da'nessa. He wasn't planning on attending, but felt he needed to get out the house. The party was held at the newly renovated Hilton Hotel. The party location was beautiful, and you can tell a lot of money was spent on this party. It had a large guest list of who's-who among the civil service workers. Everyone was there, including the city mayor. Wendy was there also, but her husband Anthony was not. Things had not gone well for Wendy and Anthony lately, and it was rumored that he had left her. Jerome tried to avoid Wendy all night, but she made herself available to him.

She catered to his every need just like before. Wendy kept bringing him beers. She knew that if he got drunk, he would not drive home. He loved his job and would do nothing to risk losing it. She also knew that Da'nessa and Jerome were having problems because he had confided in her as she had with him about her marriage. When he showed up at the party along, she knew she could work her old magic. As the night drew to an end and the guest started to leave, Wendy suggested they go into the coffee shop so they can get some coffee and sober up. Jerome agreed but didn't really want any coffee. He didn't even want to sober up. He wanted to remain tipsy so he could forget about his unhappy home life.

They sat in the coffee shop and talked. Wendy told him what was going on in her home. She shared that Anthony was never man enough for her and that the only reason she stayed was because of the kids. She knew he loved the kids and will always take care of them. Of the four kids, two of them were not his. He knew, but he didn't care.

Wendy had been his middle school sweetheart. By the time he saw her in high school, she had her oldest child who was almost two. Anthony and Wendy didn't date until their senior year of high school, and by this time, she had another child by a different daddy. Wendy was a street girl from a broken home. She did what she had to so that she could survive.

Anthony felt sorry for her and vowed to take care of her, no matter what. He was true to his word. He knew she didn't love him, but his word was his word. Anthony deserved better than her, and she knew it. She kept trying to get him to leave, but he would only look the other way. Anthony had self-esteem issues because he was short in stature. The alcohol was starting to make Jerome sick to his stomach. Wendy had a room in the hotel and offered him a place to rest until he felt better. He was resistant at first but decided to take her up on the offer. By the time they reached the room, Jerome threw up all over his clothing.

Wendy helped him undress, and he put on a hotel bathrobe. He lay on the sofa. Everything was spinning. He finally fell asleep. Wendy gathered his things and called the laundry service. They said it would take about three hours, but they could clean them. While Jerome slept, Wendy went downstairs to get another cup of espresso. She knew her friend upstairs was hurting emotionally as well as physically. She felt sad for him because she knew he loved his wife dearly. She had once hoped he would desire her. Yet, Jerome had always treated her with respect. She made advances in the past toward him, but he stopped her. He didn't sleep with married women, not even unhappy ones.

She knew the rumors about them, but none of them were true. She had never met a truer friend. The only reason she took the job transfer when he did was for the money. Most people didn't realize she had her job offer first and had signed off on the paperwork, but one of her kids got the chicken pops so she stayed home an extra two week. By this time, Jerome had accepted the other job offer.

Wendy was glad because she needed a friendly face. Besides, she had slept with other guys in the precincts, and that's why she had a bad reputation. For a woman, a bad reputation will follow you, no matter where you go. Two hours passed when she decided to go to the room and check on her friend. He was still asleep on the sofa. Wendy decided to take a shower and go to bed. She fell asleep and didn't hear the laundry service when they arrived. Jerome answered the door and paid them for the service. He felt better and decided to take a shower and go home. When he got out the shower, Wendy was awake. "How are you feeling?" she asked.

"A little better," he responded. "They brought my things, so I'm going to get dressed and leave. Thanks for everything," Jerome said.

"You are welcome. That's what friends are for," she said.

Jerome looked at Wendy, and for the first time, he saw a very lonely woman. He put on his briefs and T-shirt. Then he decided to stay and watch TV with her. He really didn't want to go home to Da'nessa and her depressed state. They both fell asleep watching TV. When Jerome woke up, Wendy was still asleep. *She is a beautiful woman,* he thought as he watched her sleep. He knew she just happened to have had a hard life growing up. He looked at her with sadness. At that moment, he knew he was vulnerable.

He was watching her body as she breathed in and out. Jerome realized Wendy had a nice body for someone with four children. She was a very light-skinned African American woman who could almost pass for a Caucasian woman. Her mother was Caucasian and her dad was African American. Jerome didn't know why, but at that moment, he decided to caress Wendy. She stirred but did not wake up. He touched her again, but this time, he leaned over and kissed her on the mouth. Wendy woke up and looked at him. She didn't stop him but wondered if she should. She had wanted this for a very long time. Jerome continued to caress her through her silk gown. Before they knew what was going on, he had advanced toward lovemaking.

His touch felt so good to her. She just could not stop him. She longed for this man so many nights, and here he was coming on to her. Wendy gave in and returned the favors. She was amazed at his body. Jerome pulled out protection from his wallet. Lately, he always kept protection in his wallet. He didn't know why or maybe he does for such a moment as this. They enjoyed one another for almost an hour. Afterward, Jerome felt guilty for cheating on his wife. As he lay there beside Wendy, Jerome saw a vision of Ma Bessie and jumped straight up out of bed. Wendy didn't know what had happened. So he lied and said that he had a leg cramp. Jerome went in the bathroom and washed up. What had he done?

He had committed adultery. How could he do this to the woman he loved with all his soul? Now he had a heart full of remorse and guilt. Now he remembered Ma Bessie's words as he sat there in the bathroom of another woman. Ma Bessie had said, "Adultery will destroy a marriage, even the appearance of adultery, but when it's your soul mate, they will forgive you. Please remember this when times get tough." At that moment, he had fear because he knew Da'nessa would never forgive him for being with Wendy. Any other woman yes, but not Wendy.

How could he ever let Da'nessa know about this? She already hated Wendy; now she will really hate both of them. He hated that Da'nessa lied to him about Michael, but now he might have to lie to her about Wendy. Jerome wondered, *Will their marriage be based on more lies?* Jerome had been in the bathroom for a while, and Wendy needed to use it. She tapped on the door. "May I come in?" she said. She had put her sleeping gown back on. They both knew that they needed to talk. It was now 8:00 a.m., and he was not ready to go home. They decided to get dressed and went downstairs to have breakfast and talk.

Jerome gave Wendy a hug and asked her to forgive him. He said he had no right to take advantage of her like he did. He said he was truly sorry. They were shown a booth near the back of the restaurant. They ordered their food, and while they waited they talk. "What's next?" Jerome said. "I've got to tell my wife. I love her with all my soul, and I know this will most likely destroy my marriage." He confessed to Wendy that Da'nessa already thought that we were sleeping together. Wendy was not surprised; she knew her reputation.

About an hour into their breakfast when they were almost done, Da'nessa walked up to the table where Jerome and Wendy sat. She looked beautiful. Her hair was combed; she had on makeup and a beautiful cream-color pant suit. She did not have Carissa with her. Jerome didn't know what to say. He and Wendy just looked at one another. They expected an ugly scene. Da'nessa surprised everyone. She said in a small still voice, "Jerome, I love you with every fiber in my body and soul. You are truly my soul mate. I don't want to know what happened last night. I don't care, and I do not want to care. If you love me and you want this marriage, you will get up now and leave with me. You will never speak to Mrs. Anthony Kramer again." Da'nessa's focus was on Jerome.

She continued to say, "Our home will return to a loving and peaceful place because we have two children who needed to see loving parents. Tyrone and Carissa are at home waiting for their father. If I mean nothing to you, than let me walk away and give me three days to pack up and move out of the house." Then she looked at Wendy and said, "I have been in your shoes, and I know what it feels like. I forgive you."

Da'nessa turned to walk away, and Jerome took her hand. He pulled her close and held her. Wendy got up from the table and walked away. Jerome gave the waiter thirty dollars to cover the cost of breakfast and a nice tip. When they got outside, Da'nessa broke down into tears, she felt so bad for the way she had treated the man she loved. She had driven him to this, and she had no one to blame but herself. She knew that she had Jerome's heart, and she knew her heart belonged to him. They never spoke of that day or Michael again. Da'nessa trusted her husband and will always trust him.

JOURNAL 18

Through the Valley of the Shadow of Death

The Lord is close to the brokenhearted; He
rescues those whose spirits are crushed.

—Psalm 34:18 (NLT)

Today, August 3, is Caressa's thirteenth birthday. She is a teenager. Da'nessa was also turning forty-three today. Tyrone has finished college and working in his degree field. Tyrone also has his own place. Where did the years go? Da'nessa thought.

The party planning had been going on for weeks. A thirteenth birthday is a pretty big deal. Jerome spared no expense for his baby girl. She wanted a princess party, and he gave her one. He even had a princess throne built on the dance floor in their backyard. Caressa wore a beautiful pink dress, and she even wore a crown. There were about sixty people at the party, including Tyrone and his new girlfriend. Her name is Mirabelle Littlejohn. She is of Indian and Caucasian persuasion. She is a really nice girl, and Tyrone seemed to like her a lot. His dad was little skeptical about the relationship. He wanted him to stay focused on his career for a while and build up his savings account.

Tyrone loved and respected his dad, but the only opinion that mattered was his mommy Da'nessa's. Her approval meant the most. Tyrone still loved Da'nessa dearly, and her opinion meant everything. Da'nessa and Jerome had fallen in love all over again. They completed their marriage counseling session and agreed to no more secrets. They learned to love and respect one another. Even their lovemaking was still magical. Everything was as it should be in the world of love and happiness.

September 9, their whole world turned upside down. It was a cold, wet, rainy morning. Da'nessa felt a chill in her bones. Caressa was ill today. It was the start of her menstrual cycle, and she was cramping. Her mother decided to let her stay home in bed. Caressa took some pain pills and went back to sleep.

Da'nessa was teaching her class and was about to administer a test. The room was so quiet to the point where you can hear a pin drop. There was a knock at the door of her classroom. Da'nessa opened the door. It was an office assistant. She told Da'nessa she was needed in the principal's office and that she would stay with the kids in the classroom. Da'nessa thought that this was unusual. Maybe it was Caressa, and she needs to go home and see about her. Da'nessa walked into the principal's office. She saw Jerome's boss, Steven Schmidt, and another uniformed officer; she knew something was wrong. Her body started to shake. "Has Jerome been in an accident?" she asked. Steven asked her to please sit down; Da'nessa started to cry. She knew what it meant to be asked to sit down.

"Is Jerome okay?" she asked in a more persistent voice.

"Jerome was in an accident," his boss said. "He was killed." The words came out slow and painful. Da'nessa had hoped she misunderstood him. There is no way her husband is no longer breathing and walking around on this earth. As she tried to focus on the moment, she heard him continue to speak, saying, "He was pronounced dead at nine o'clock in the morning."

She couldn't move. Her body would not move. Did he say her husband and soul mate was dead? Da'nessa began to cry uncontrollably. Everyone in the office had tears in their eyes. Steven held her while she cried. The pain was unbearable. Jerome was the love of her life, her best friend; he was everything to her. How could he be dead? They had plans to retire and travel in a few years. They were going to visit all the national parks. Now he was gone forever. Da'nessa could not grasp reality. She had to see his body. She needed to touch him to know for herself that he was no longer breathing.

She was hoping this was some kind of sick joke. They had just made love this morning. He even suggested to stay home in bed and watch cartoons. She would have, but her class had their state placement exams today. Because Jerome was a police officer, she knew she had to call his mother before word of his death hit the television news. The news media had been told to wait until next of kin was notified. Da'nessa called Tyrone and broke the news to him. She asked him to meet her at the morgue to see the body.

Tyrone was stunned. He and Mirabelle agreed to meet her. Mirabelle drove because Tyrone was too upset to drive. He was really concerned about his little sister because no one had told her yet. She was at home sleeping. Da'nessa then called Vernita, Jerome's mother. She screamed in agony. Da'nessa also called Jerome's uncle in Middletown and asked him to go and be with Vernita. At the morgue, they explained to them that Jerome was in pursuit of a car when a truck driver ran a red light and broadsided his squad car. The car flipped over three times. His neck was broken, and he died instantly.

They allowed the family a few minutes to be with the body. She held on to him and cried. Why did he leave her so soon? They had too many plans. How would she raise their daughter without him? Then she remembered she needs to get home to Caressa before the media made it there. She had not told Caressa yet. She rode home with Tyrone and Mirabelle. When they told Caressa, she screamed in bitter pain. She wanted her daddy to come home. *Why didn't the other guy die instead of her daddy?* thought Caressa. She was so upset, and the only person she would allow to comfort her was Tyrone. She loved her brother, and she needed him more than ever. She and Tyrone sat in her dad's favorite recliner and cried.

Da'nessa called her family in Georgia and told them what had happened. Here she was, a forty-three-year-old widow. Word about Jerome's death quickly became the topic of the local news. Their home phone rang off the hook. The family decided to change the answering service to say, "Thank you for your concerns and sympathy, but the family needs time to grieve such an unexpected loss." No one would be able to leave a message. By 6:00 p.m., the house was full of relatives and close family friends. Vernita and some of the other family members had arrived from Middletown.

When word of his death got out, the neighbors brought over food and other needful items for the family. Da'nessa was really starting to feel overwhelmed. Her doctor had called in a prescription, just a little something to calm her nerves. She took them, but there was no relief. The love of her life will never again walk through that door, and she didn't know what to do with all that pain. Da'nessa went to her bedroom to lie down. Caressa joined her, and together they lay there and cried. Caressa finally fell asleep, but Da'nessa could not sleep. Everything in that bedroom reminded her of Jerome. She could still smell his scent. Her heart ached. She had not felt pain like this since she lost Ma Bessie fourteen years ago.

Da'nessa was glad to have people in the house. She really didn't want her and Caressa be there alone with all these memories. She finally dozed off to sleep. While she slept, Da'nessa had a dream. She was walking along a white sandy beach. Just like the ones back on Guam. She was the only one on the beach, and it was sunset. She remembered she always liked the beach when it was nearly empty. As she walked along the beach, she could hear the sounds of the ocean and the birds flying overhead. She could also smell and taste ocean salt in the air. The dream was so real. Then she saw it, a familiar sight. She saw the small outcrop of rocks she used to visit on Taugra Beach in Guam. How could she be in Guam?

Da'nessa felt a peace that she could not explain. She walked over to her old spot, and that was when she saw them. There they were sitting on her old blanket laughing and talking. It was Jerome and Ma Bessie. "How did you two get here?" she asked. Jerome spoke first. He said all he remembers is chasing a car on Ocean Avenue and Montauk when he heard a loud crash. Then he saw Ma Bessie reaching out and taking his hand. He then felt peace, and real peace, like he never felt before.

Next, he and Ma Bessie were on the beach. He said Ma Bessie told him that they needed to wait on Da'nessa before heading into the light. So they decided to wait in one of your favorite places. Da'nessa has never told Jerome about the rocks at Taugra Beach. How did he know this information? Ma Bessie smiled at her baby but never said a word. Jerome was not aware that he had died on earth. Da'nessa knew in her soul that she had to tell him and release him. It was difficult, and she was not ready to share such sad information. Yet, she knew better than to keep things from him.

"Jerome," Da'nessa said, "you died this morning at 9:00 a.m. You were in your squad car on a chase when someone ran the red light and hit your car. Ma Bessie is here to help you cross over."

Jerome looked at her with sadness in his eyes. He told her that he had a conflict. He was at peace, and yet how can he have peace knowing that he will not be with them on earth? Da'nessa realized that she too had peace. She knew that he didn't suffer and that Ma Bessie will look after him as she had done for her while she was alive on earth.

Da'nessa knew in her heart that we all have an appointed time on earth. Jerome's time had ended, but his love and his spirit lived on in his wife and children. From that point forward, she knew that the family will be okay. Ma Bessie took Jerome's hand and finally spoke. She said to Jerome, "It's time."

There was a strong breeze in the air, and everything smelled of sea salt. Jerome's last words to Da'nessa were, "I will love you forever, and I will love you for always." That was a special quote from Caressa's favorite childhood book by author Robert Munsch, *Love You Forever*. Da'nessa started to cry again. She felt a gentle tug on her hand when she realized she had awakened to the soft tug of Caressa. "Mom, are you okay? You are crying in your sleep," said her baby. Then Caressa said the strangest thing. "Mom, do you smell the ocean?" Da'nessa smelled the ocean, and she could taste sea salt on her lips. Da'nessa knew then that her visit with Jerome was real. It was very real, and she found comfort in their final visit.

JOURNAL 19

Life Goes on Regardless of the Pain

And the peace of God, which surpasses all understanding,
will guard your hearts and mind in Christ Jesus.

—Philippians 4:7

The years flew by, and Caressa was graduating from high school. It had been almost five years since her father's untimely death. She missed him dearly, but her mom missed him even more. Caressa continued to be a good child and a strong support for her mother Da'nessa. Tyrone had remained in their lives as well. He loved his sister and stepmother. Tyrone married Mirabelle Littlejohn. They were very happy together.

Caressa had started dating as well. She had attended her high school prom with Brian Tyson. He is the star quarterback for their high school football team. Brian had received a full athletic scholarship to play football at Georgia Tech University in Atlanta, Georgia. It's a great school with an outstanding sports department. Caressa had applied to Spelman College in Atlanta, Georgia and was accepted.

Da'nessa was happy for Caressa and would never do anything to hold her back from following her dreams or the man she cared about. Caressa had second thoughts about leaving her mother and the state of Connecticut. She was worried about her mom. She seemed lonely to Caressa. Da'nessa never dated after her husband died. Not one date in five years, although she was still a very beautiful woman.

It's not that she didn't have offers and opportunities. She always turned them down. Jerome Leary was her soul mate. Da'nessa felt that she could never give her heart in that manner again, so why waste another man's time and energy? It would not be fair to him. Da'nessa felt that she had a full and complete life. She was blessed to have truly loved a wonderful man, and she helped raise two fantastic kids. What more could a woman ask?

Four years of college flew by, and Caressa was due to graduate in May. Da'nessa was busy making plans to attend her baby girl's college graduation. She made hotel reservations at the "W" Hotel in downtown Atlanta, and she also reserved a connecting room for her parents who were meeting her there. Tyrone and Mirabelle would join them at the ceremony; they were staying with one of his fraternity brother and wife in the Atlanta area.

Everyone was proud of Caressa, including the love of her life Brian Tyson. Brian was also graduating from college and had several offers to play professional football. Caressa loved Atlanta and hoped that Brian would accept the offer from the Atlanta Falcons. She did not express her desires either way. She wanted it to be his decision because she was willing to follow him wherever he chose.

Graduation day came and went. It was a beautiful ceremony. They had also attended Brian's graduation. Brian told Caressa that he wanted to stay in Atlanta and play football. She was really pleased with his decision. Brian knew secretly that Caressa wanted him to stay in Atlanta, but he made her think that the decision was totally his. He too liked Atlanta. Once Brian signed his lucrative contract with the Falcons, he proposed to Caressa, and she happily accepted.

Brian and Caressa decided they wanted to get married in Atlanta. They had purchased a beautiful home in the Alpharetta area of Atlanta. Their home had a large yard, and they felt that a lovely wedding at their new home was what both of them wanted. They hired the best wedding coordinator that money could buy in the Atlanta area. She lived up to her reputation. She transformed their beautiful six-bedroom home into a luxury work of art. The guest list was just as impressive.

They had invited a hundred relatives and close friends, and all had accepted the invite. As the guests arrived, they were met with valet parking. Da'nessa was impressed with the number of famous people her daughter and new son-in-law knew. It was time for the ceremony. Da'nessa had missed the rehearsal dinner. Her doctor would not release her to fly due to a nasty ear infection. Luckily, the medication worked, and she was cleared to fly. She flew in the morning of the ceremony. Caressa had assured her that all the plans were coming together and for her not to worry: just rest and get well.

The home was transformed into the most elegant chapel. The usher waited to escort the mother of the bride to her seat. *It is so beautiful,* Da'nessa thought. Their colors were cream and gold. They used the same colors as her and Jerome's wedding. Caressa had also chosen calla lilies as her main flowers. She knew her mother loved calla lilies. Da'nessa walked with her escort down the center to the front of the parlor, which had been transformed into a beautiful sanctuary. Da'nessa was impressed by the guest list, which included other famous athletes, actors, actress, elected officials. She was busy looking around and admiring all of them when she noticed him. Her heart skipped a beat. He was older, but she knew it was him.

Da'nessa could not believe her eyes. She looked a second time. It can't be him, and if it is him, how did he get invited. His name was not on the guest list. She would have noticed. Da'nessa felt herself getting jittery and weak in the knees. How much farther to that seat, she thought. Brian and the officiating minister came and stood near the makeshift altar, which signaled the arrival of the bride. Then he noticed her. He couldn't believe his eyes. He had not attended the practice run of the wedding because he was out of town. He had his assistant stand in and film the rehearsal. He reasoned in his mind. She is still beautiful to him. She looked as if she had not aged one day.

Here, they both were in the same room. Had fate dealt him such a lucky hand? Pastor Rupert Latimore was officiating Da'nessa's daughter's wedding. Da'nessa felt weird, and she wondered if he remembered her. Rupert stood trying to appear strong, but his knees were weak and his heart pounded. Was this really her, was this really his Da'nessa? Years had passed since they last saw one another, but he could never forget her. She was the only woman he has ever loved other than Cynthia. The bridal song played as Caressa walked down the aisle. She looked beautiful as Tyrone escorted her to the front where Brian stood waiting. "Who gives this woman away to be married?" said Rupert as part of the ceremony. "I do and her mother," said Tyrone, and then he took his seat between Da'nessa and Mirabelle. Caressa also added a special touch to the wedding ceremony. She and her mother lit a candle for her father whom she felt was there in the spirit.

Rupert did a great job officiating the wedding. Everything was on schedule and exactly as Brian and Caressa wanted it. After the ceremony, Rupert approached Da'nessa. "Hello, Da'nessa, it is so wonderful to see you," he said. Da'nessa responded by saying, "Hello, Rupert, it's nice to see you," as she blushed. "You are just as beautiful as I remember," he commented. "Your daughter looks like you, and she is such a lovely young lady," said Rupert. "Thank you," Da'nessa said. She was at a loss of words. How could this be? She has not seen this man in years, and here he stands having officiated her baby girl's wedding.

Caressa was looking for her mother to take pictures. She found her talking to Pastor Latimore. "Excuse me, Pastor, but we need you and my mother for a picture," said Caressa. After several pictures and meeting other guests, it was time to move to the tent for the reception. Pastor Rupert had not planned on staying for the reception, but now that he had reunited with Da'nessa, there was no way he could leave. He had to know everything about her life. He missed her. It had been too many years. He refused to lose her again. He didn't care if she had someone in her life. He was determined he would be a part of her life, if only as a friend. Da'nessa also wondered about Rupert. Was Cynthia at home waiting for him? What about his twin boys? Where were they?

Rupert did not allow coy to get in his way. He approached Da'nessa and asked if he could talk with her. She had not been introduced to all the guests that Brian and Caressa wanted her to meet, but she promised as soon as she was done, they can talk. He was happy that she had not shunned his request, and he was more than willing to wait. She was worth it. He waited this long, so what's another hour?

Caressa saw her mom talking to the pastor a second time and finally asked if they knew one another. "Yes, we know one another," said Da'nessa. "We knew each other from Guam." Caressa thought this is great. She knew Pastor Rupert, and she liked him. Caressa had attended some of his Sunday services. She also knew he was divorced, and several women were unable to trap him. He was a prize catch that no single woman was able to catch. He had an excellent reputation in the community. This pleased Caressa, and she wished she had thought of introducing them long before now. She knew her mom had dated no one in all these years since the death of her father. She wanted her mother to live her life to the fullest. She felt that a part of her mother died with her dad. As much as she loved her father, he was not coming back, and her mom was very much alive and deserved to be love.

Caressa turned and told Brian about her mother and Pastor Rupert. "Let's make sure they are seated next to one another at the reception," she said. Brian called an attendant and asked him to rearrange the seat cards so that Pastor Rupert was sitting next to his mother-in-law. After the meet and greet, everyone went into the reception to have their meal.

Rupert and Da'nessa found their seat and realized they were seated next to one another. They both looked at her daughter, and Da'nessa knew it was Caressa's doing. Caressa just smiled at her mom and winked her eye. Da'nessa loved that child and was once again very pleased with her and the wonderful blessings her life had given her.

Da'nessa thought about Jerome and wished he could be there. Deep in her soul, she felt that he was there looking down and smiling at all he had help to create. Rupert turned to Da'nessa and spoke softly. "I have missed you all these years. I wondered what happened to you. I knew you went to Orlando, Florida. After that, I lost touch with anyone who knew you," Rupert confessed.

"How is Cynthia?" Da'nessa asked. "Cynthia is well," he responded. "We are divorced. We have been divorced for seven years."

"I'm sorry to hear that," said Da'nessa. Rupert told her, "Don't be concerned over it. It's what she wanted. She had a difficult time after the twins were born." Rupert turned and motioned to a tall good-looking young man. "I would like to introduce you to my son Dalyn Latimore. He is a twin. His brother Jalyn is working in Japan." Da'nessa was impressed with his son. He is a polite and good-looking young man. He looked so much like his father.

Rupert continued, "Anyway, Cynthia hated being a mother. She had no love in her for the boys. At first, we thought it was post-partum, so she went to counseling;" He shared that Cynthia confessed that she had the boys only to please him and that she really never wanted kids. Cynthia admitted that she was self-centered. She tried to be there physically and emotionally for them, but finally she moved out one day. "It took me three years to get her to sign the divorce papers," said Rupert.

Rupert continued by saying that Cynthia told him she was hoping that one day she would wake up and want to be a mother and wife. It never happened. She was married to her career. Rupert and the boys got orders back to the United States. He had custody of the boys, so they came home with him, and Cynthia remained in Guam. She tried to keep in touch with them, but her heart was not in it. Their extended family was not surprised by her actions. They knew a side of her Rupert didn't know. Regardless, Rupert knew he was blessed to have those boys.

"My boys turned out well, and they are both successful and living happy lives," he commented. "One is married, and the other one is enjoying the single life and traveling. Neither is in the ministry." Rupert wasn't boasting; he was just proud of them.

Da'nessa hated that she had asked, and it showed on her facial expressions. Rupert reassured her it was okay. He also expressed to Da'nessa that he was sorry to hear about the loss of her husband. "Thanks," she said. Then she explained that he was killed when Caressa was thirteen years old. He was a police officer killed in the line of duty. "You never remarried," he asked. "No," she replied.

"Are you dating anyone?" Rupert inquired. Da'nessa looked at Rupert and smiled. She had not dated anyone since her husband's death. When he died, he took her heart with him. She said in a soft voice, "No, I have dated no one since his death." Rupert then replied, "I'm so sorry to hear that. I can understand a broken heart. When you left Guam, I felt a big hole in my heart. It was torn down the middle, and it hurt beyond measure." She looked at him in amazement. "I didn't think I could love again," he confessed.

"I stayed with Cynthia out of obligation more so than love. I was shocked when she got pregnant. We had not discussed this. She felt she needed to have a baby to save the marriage." Rupert continued to speak, "When she discovered it was twins she was really mad. She only wanted one but now she had to share with two. After she left, I never dated anyone."

Rupert continued to confess, "I thought of you every day. I included you in my daily prayers. I asked the Lord to close my eyes to all other women except you. I promised God that once I saw you, if you were happily married then, I would move on."

Da'nessa was speechless by his comments. Rupert continued to tell it all. He said, "Woman in the church are bold, and many tried to date me, but I refused to date. Some even rumored that I'm gay, but I knew the truth, and I didn't care what they thought. I searched for you all over Orlando. Then I decided to go to your hometown in South Georgia," said Rupert. "I met Ma Bessie." Da'nessa was shocked and surprised. No one told her that he had visited Adel. Her parents confirmed that he had visited, but because she was married, there was no reason to tell her of the visit. Rupert shared the details of his visit.

When he sat with Ma Bessie, she shared the following with him. "She told me that you were married, but there would come a day when you would need me. She said you were happily married and that I should give up pursuing you. She also said life would bring us together when it was time. In my heart of hearts, I knew she was right," said Rupert. "I had peace, and I made a decision not to date anyone. I would wait until we meet again," he said this with water midst in his eyes.

Rupert then said, "I had no clue it would be today. Yet, I smelled the ocean today, and I had the taste of salt on my tongue palate this morning." Da'nessa thought this was strange because she had the same sensation this morning, and she was sure it was side effects from the ear infection medication. Da'nessa knew that Rupert spoke the truth. They had a lot to talk about, and they talked for hours. Rupert invited Da'nessa to his church service on Sunday. It's a lovely church with about two thousand members. Rupert introduced Da'nessa to the church members as his very special friend that he had not seen in years. It was clear there were some jealous women in that church. One lady got up and walked out of church in a huff. Some people giggled because they knew she had been trying to hook the pastor.

Da'nessa's visit in Atlanta passed quickly, and it was time for her to fly back to Connecticut. Brian and Caressa were still on their honeymoon. Rupert did not want her to leave. He asked if he could come to Connecticut for a visit. Da'nessa knew that Rupert had strong feelings for her. She cared about him too, but she was confused. She felt as though she was wrong to care for another man. Jerome was her heart, and she still loved him very much.

Da'nessa asked Rupert to give her time to think. They did exchange phone numbers, and she promised to keep in touch. When she returned home, Da'nessa talked with Tyrone about Rupert. She told him how they had met in Guam and that he was married at the time. She was very truthful with Tyrone. Tyrone knew that Da'nessa loved his father, but he wanted her to live her life. At times he felt that she died the day his father was killed. He did not want that mundane existence for her. He was concerned she would never date again.

Tyrone told Da'nessa that she should not fear loving again. She had been a loving and respectful wife to his father, but it wasn't fair to live her life locked in the past. She loved her son, and she appreciated his advice, but she still had mixed emotions. That night, Da'nessa fell asleep and was awakened to the sound of the ocean. Da'nessa sat up in her bed. She knew she heard the sounds of the ocean. The room was completely dark, which was really unusual because Da'nessa always kept a nightlight on in the bathroom, but even that was off. Da'nessa thought to herself that the power was out.

She lay back down and dozed off to sleep, only to be awakened again. Once more, she heard the sound of the ocean, and she smelled sea salt. Da'nessa looked at the wall in front of her as it opened up to reveal a beach. It was a beautiful white sand beach. Da'nessa saw someone walking toward her on the beach. She thought the person was carrying a volleyball.

She started to laugh within because she remembered how she met Rupert on the beach over a volleyball. As the individual approached her, she realized it was Jerome carrying the volleyball on the beach. He walked up to her. He didn't speak, but she heard him in her mind. He handed her the ball and said, "It's okay, my love. Take it and move on with your life. I am okay, and I will always love you."

Then he turned her around and pointed her in the other direction. She saw someone else standing on the other end of the beach. She wanted to stay there with Jerome forever and not move, but Jerome gave her a nudge. As she moved toward the other person, he was coming toward her. She knew it was Rupert. He walked up to her and asked, "Is that my volleyball?" And when she open her mouth, she spoke and could hear her voice for the first time since the vision began. She responded with a "Yes, this is your volleyball." When she turned back around, Jerome was gone and Rupert was holding her hand. Rupert looked deep into her soul and said everything will be all right. Da'nessa knew he was right.

She awoke from her vision in tears. Da'nessa knew the dream was symbolic. She knew that Ma Bessie had predicted everything correctly; she picked up her phone and called Rupert. It was 3:33 a.m.

Rupert woke from his dream and answered the phone. "Hello, Rupert, it's me," Da'nessa said.

"Is everything okay?" he asked in a panic.

"Yes, Rupert, it is okay," she said. "I just call to say I love you." Rupert felt tears roll down his eyes. "I love you too, Da'nessa. I was just dreaming about you," he said. "We were on the beach, and you gave me a volleyball. There on the beach, I asked you if you loved me. You looked deep into my eyes and was about to speak when the phone rang, and I woke up." Rupert was amazed and continued, "Now here you are on the phone answering my question. God has answered my all my prayers."

Rupert wasted no time asking that special question, "Da'nessa, will you marry me? I don't ever want to have you out of my life. Truthfully, I do not want to spend another day without you in my life. I knew it years ago when I met you that you were my soul mate."

Da'nessa thought as he spoke, was this possible could she have two soul mates? She had felt a special connection to him years ago, and she knew at that moment it was just as strong today as it was years ago. Da'nessa accepted Rupert's proposal, and they were married in a small private ceremony. She is now the wife of Pastor Rupert Latimore and First Lady Da'nessa Latimore of Greater Baptist Church, Atlanta, Georgia. This is the ending of the recorded journal of a first lady. Then again, who knows? There is always excitement in the church.

The morale of the story is doing things your way instead of God's way will always result in hurt and pain. Delay gratification because you know God's will is the only way to save yourself a lot of pain and heartache. His will be done. Remember Romans 13:10 (TLB): "Love does no wrong to anyone. That's why it fully satisfies all of God's requirements. It is the only law you need." Lastly, Romans 8:5 (TLB): "Those who let themselves be controlled by their lower natures live only to please themselves, but those who follow after the Holy Spirit find themselves doing those things that please God."

ABOUT THE AUTHOR

C. D. Covington is an aspiring writer. She is a military veteran and currently works for the government. C. D. Covington loves the written word and has an extensive collections of journals. She also credits herself with having a superactive imagination. C. D. Covington is a Christian who loves serving God, her church, and the local community. She is also a blogger. She and her family currently resides in the Atlanta, Georgia, area.

CPSIA information can be obtained
at www.ICGtesting.com
Printed in the USA
LVHW110843070720
659732LV00004BA/288